TRAIL FROM TAOS

"Señor, why does this man never speak?"

The jailer glanced at Never-Speaks and back to Red Feather, his expression dark and foreboding.

"Because he is wiser than you. And because he has no tongue. He lost it by using it too much. It would be best to remember that."

It was the longest speech that any jailer had ever given, and certainly the most significant. Red Feather recoiled in shock. The other prisoner had had his tongue cut out, for using it too much.

This put an immediate end to attempts at communication, but spurred renewed activity at the barred window. Finally there came the night when White Fox roused his father excitedly.

"The iron bar! It is free!" he whispered.

Red Feather jumped up to feel the lower end of the bar in the predawn darkness. Yes, it was true. The bar could now be raised high enough in the upper socket to clear the sill at the bottom. Now, if only they could bend it.

"We will wait," Red Feather whispered. "It is too near light."

He pointed to the yellow glow along the eastern horizon.

"Tonight," he told his son.

Bantam Books by Don Coldsmith
Ask your bookseller for the books you have missed

Trail From Taos

DON COLDSMITH

BANTAM BOOKS
NEW YORK · TORONTO · LONDON · SYDNEY · AUCKLAND

All of the characters in this book are fictitious, and any resemblance to actual persons, living or dead, is purely coincidental.

*This edition contains the complete text
of the original hardcover edition.*
NOT ONE WORD HAS BEEN OMITTED.

TRAIL FROM TAOS
A Bantam Book / published by arrangement with Doubleday

PRINTING HISTORY
Doubleday edition published April 1989
Bantam edition / October 1990

ISBN 0-553-28760-5

Published simultaneously in the United States and Canada

Bantam Books are published by Bantam Books, a division of
Bantam Doubleday Dell Publishing Group, Inc. Its trademark,
consisting of the words "Bantam Books" and the portrayal of a
rooster, is Registered in U.S. Patent and Trademark Office and in
other countries. Marca Registrada. Bantam Books, 666 Fifth
Avenue, New York, New York 10103.

PRINTED IN THE UNITED STATES OF AMERICA

RAD   0 9 8 7 6 5 4 3 2 1

Number 14 of the Spanish Bit Saga
Time period: 1680, about twenty years after
The Flower in the Mountains

Trail
From
Taos

»»»»»»»»»»»»

1

» » »

Red Feather led his caravan over the crest of the ridge and paused to let the horses blow after the steep ascent. It was a good place to stop and rest, and to become accustomed to the spectacular scene that stretched below. It was familiar, after the almost yearly expedition to Santa Fe to trade, yet always different. And, of course, so very different from the lush tallgrass prairie of home.

It seemed only a short while ago that he had stood at his father's side on this ridge and first experienced the sight of the plain below. He smiled to himself at the memory of that trip. He had been so young, so naïve. His inexperience had nearly gotten him killed. He looked back over his shoulder and waved to his wife. Moonflower smiled and waved back, then kneed her horse forward to join him. It had been her stubborn refusal to let him die that had saved him.

Now, many winters later, their own children were nearly grown. Moonflower had decided to accompany the pack train, to visit her people at the pueblo while the others went on into Santa Fe to trade.

It was a good season, he thought with satisfaction.

The pack train, laden with furs and tanned robes, numbered sixteen pack animals, not counting those they were riding. This was the largest trading venture ever attempted by the People, he believed, and he was proud to lead it. The young men learned well.

He watched Swallow and Yellow Robe move from one horse to another, checking packs and cinches. Their allies, the Head Splitters from the shortgrass country to the west of the People, had always joined in the annual expedition. There was old Turkey Foot, who had been on the very first expedition. The younger Head Splitters, Red Dog and Bull's Horn, were also rapidly becoming skilled at packing and handling the horses.

Moonflower now reined in beside him, her face shining with excitement.

"You look happy," he observed, teasing her. "What is the matter, woman, you are not tired from the journey?"

Moonflower smiled, the smile he loved to see, which crinkled the little lines at the corners of her eyes.

"Of course I am happy," she chided. "I am going home."

"You are leaving me?" he asked in mock alarm.

She laughed, showing even white teeth. She was still beautiful, Red Feather thought, even though they were both well past thirty winters.

"You cannot get rid of me so easily," she warned.

It was an exchange of long standing between them. He knew that it had been difficult for her, living far away from her home and her family, among customs unfamiliar to her. He had tried to let her know by this good-natured bantering that he understood. It had become a game between them, an open statement of respect for each other's feelings. It had helped to make theirs a happy lodge.

"My parents grow older," Moonflower said more seriously.

Red Feather nodded. Moonflower had not seen her people for several seasons. Blue Corn, his wife's father, had seemed old when first they met. He was a chief, the leader of the small pueblo a day's ride from the town of Santa Fe. Chiefs of Moonflower's people, Red Feather knew, held somewhat different status from chiefs of the buffalo hunters of the prairie. There was much that he did not understand about it. Sometimes it seemed to him that Blue Corn's position as leader of his cluster of earthen lodges held very little actual meaning. The major decisions were guided principally by the medicine men.

Yet somehow, Blue Corn did hold a place of respect that was unique in his village. His was a calm, quiet dignity, an inner strength. He asked for no trouble, and gave none. Blue Corn's people had survived for many generations in this location beside the great Southwest Trail, by tolerance of all who passed. He was known to the Spanish military patrols who made this village the northernmost point of their circuit. The soldiers were tolerant of Blue Corn's village and its people, because no trouble had ever occurred there.

At the same time, he had maintained good relations with the militant reactionaries over the mountain at the Taos pueblo. There was a nucleus of fiery anti-Spanish sentiment there which had seemed to be growing the past few seasons.

When the People first came to trade, a generation ago, Blue Corn had befriended the strangers from the prairie, given them directions, traded supplies. He possessed great wisdom, but seldom shared it unless it was asked. To Red Feather, the man had always seemed a solid dependable rock in the midst of a strange and unfamiliar landscape. No, not like a rock. Like a great tree, perhaps. But that did not quite fit, either.

Red Feather had been walking with Blue Corn one morning after a storm, a few seasons ago. The travelers had seen the approach of Rain Maker, and heard the rumble of his drum across the distant mountains. They had hurried to reach the shelter of Blue Corn's pueblo before the storm struck. The next morning, the two men had walked beside the rushing stream that was usually a dry and sandy bed. They came to a giant cottonwood which had been split and shattered by the force of the wind, and lay broken, half of it prostrate on the ground. Red Feather had remarked that the willows along the creek had fared better.

"Ah, yes," Blue Corn observed. "The willows bend as far as they must, while the cottonwood stands firm."

"I do not understand, Uncle."

"Look!" the older man advised. "By bending, they do not break. The willows will be here after the mighty cottonwood is broken."

"It is better, then," Red Feather answered, "that they bend to avoid breaking?"

Blue Corn shrugged, a twinkle in his eye.

"If you are a willow," he observed mischievously.

That, Red Feather finally decided, was the secret of Blue Corn's success. He was flexible. Like the willow, he would bend to avoid being broken, and would thus succeed. In this way he had maintained the respect and good will of the Spanish, the militant faction of his own people, and the traders from the plains. Through the years Red Feather had an increasing respect for the wisdom of this remarkable man.

"Let us move on," Red Feather announced after they had rested for a little while.

The pack train stirred into motion and began to file down the south slope of the ridge. The trail was plain, and the pack horses so well accustomed to the routine by this time that they made no effort at all to stray.

It was still several sleeps before they neared the village that had been Moonflower's home. She became more and more excited, and finally one morning, could stand it no longer.

"Could we ride ahead, my husband? I long to see my father and mother."

Red Feather smiled. There was no reason to object. The trail was plain, and there were no enemies in the entire area.

"Of course!" he agreed. "Turkey Foot can lead the pack train."

He loped back to confer with Turkey Foot, and quickly returned.

"It is good!" he reported with a smile. "Let us go!"

They cantered ahead. Moonflower, who had been completely unfamiliar with horses at the time they married, had learned rapidly. She now enjoyed the freedom of travel that the plains customs of her husband's tribe demanded. Their entire lives were centered around the buffalo and the horse. So it happened that they moved rapidly ahead of the pack train and reached the pueblo nearly half a day in advance.

Moonflower's parents came from the doorway to greet them as they approached. She kneed the horse forward, jumping down to run and embrace her mother.

"Where are the children?" the older woman asked. "Are they not with you?"

"Only White Fox," Moonflower explained. "He is a half-day behind us, with the pack train. Elk Woman has her own lodge."

"He is old enough to do this?" the boy's grandmother marveled.

"He thinks so," Moonflower laughed. "He felt that he was needed to help while we came on ahead."

Red Feather was exchanging greetings with his father-in-law.

"You have had a good journey?" Blue Corn inquired.

"Yes, Uncle. We have traveled well. And our furs are prime. Our best packs yet."

He paused, noting a lack of enthusiasm on the part of the other man. Something must be wrong.

"Uncle," he ventured, "what is it? Is it not well with you?"

Blue Corn heaved a deep sigh of resignation. He nodded gently.

"With us, yes. It is not that, my son. But these are troubled times."

"Trouble?" Red Feather blurted.

"Yes. You know it has been coming. Blood has been shed. It may not be possible for you to trade in Santa Fe."

2
» » »

"Yes, these are troubled times," Blue Corn was saying.

The travelers had rested and eaten, and now the two men walked along the stream to talk. Red Feather had come to look forward to these visits, short and infrequent though they might be. There was something of stability in the way Blue Corn walked the sandy path that he had walked since childhood. Something of immortality, it seemed. It had taken much understanding on the part of the young Red Feather. It was almost beyond his comprehension that these lodges of earthen bricks had stood in one spot for many generations. The lodges of the People were moved with the seasons, migrating with the buffalo and then choosing a desirable area in which to winter. Here, there was inescapable sameness.

They passed the rotting stump of the giant cottonwood which had been the subject of a conversation long ago. Red Feather saw, a few paces away, a sapling as tall as his head. Its leaves quivered in the breeze, and he wondered idly how long it would be until this sturdy newcomer would become a tree which could replace the shady canopy of the dead giant. More generations. How many generations of Blue Corn's people had seen these trees grow to maturity, shade their children, fall into the silver-gray of death and decay, and then be replaced?

In a way, he realized, it was much like the yearly cycle of the grass. The long nights of winter were followed by the Moon of Awakening, and the greening of the new grass. Then the buffalo would return to eat, grow fat, and be harvested by the People and their four-legged brothers. The Moon of Falling Leaves would signal the last phase, with the grasses going dormant and the buffalo disappearing for the winter. The People would enter winter camp, to wait for the cycle to repeat next season.

Of course, Blue Corn's people of the pueblo lived by a yearly cycle of growing crops, too. But Red Feather was just beginning to understand the timelessness of their way of life. The pueblo's lodges had been there for many winters, their spirit renewed by each generation in turn. Just as the children of each generation had been shaded at play by new generations of cottonwoods.

"What will you do now?" Blue Corn asked.

Red Feather looked up in surprise.

"Go to Santa Fe," he stated flatly. "We have come to trade!"

Blue Corn, never one to argue, nodded tentatively, then spoke again.

"It may be dangerous."

"I think not, Uncle. Look, we have always been friends of the Spanish, since my father and Sky-Eyes began the trading."

Blue Corn nodded again.

"But," he pointed out, "those who hate the Spanish may object to your trading with them."

"Your people?"

"Yes. My people have been badly treated, many generations. You remember Popé, the Elder from the Tewas?"

Red Feather nodded.

"He saved my life when I was wounded."

"He is back in Taos. You knew he had been in prison in Santa Fe?"

"But was he not released last year?"

Blue Corn nodded.

"Yes, but he is bitter. When he was caged, you know, several others were beaten. Three Elders were killed with the rope."

Blue Corn's eyes reflected the horror of such a death by hanging. Their spirits would be unable to escape the body, he explained, because of the constriction of the rope around the neck.

"*Aiee!*" Red Feather murmured. "What is Popé doing in Taos?"

"He is stirring up the young men to resist the Spanish," Blue Corn explained. "It is a thing of the spirit."

"I do not understand, Uncle."

"The Spanish elders, you know, the ones who wear this sign"—he paused to trace a cross in the sand with his finger—"they tell the young that our ways are bad."

"But why, Uncle? Why would they do that?"

Blue Corn shrugged.

"I do not know. I have noticed this myself. They want to tell their story, but will listen to no one else's."

"Theirs is a good story," observed Red Feather.

"That of First Man and First Woman, and the real-snake. Also, that part about the chief who rises from the dead."

"A good story," Blue Corn agreed. "But why, then, do they not wish to listen to ours, or yours?"

Both shook their heads in nonunderstanding. It would be only polite to exchange creation legends around the story fires. This was an expected form of entertainment among both the People and those of the pueblos. To encounter a tribe who refused to listen . . . *aiee!*

"Well," Blue Corn continued, "Popé, you remember, has always been worried that the Spanish want our young people to give up the old ways. The prayers, the ceremonies, the spirit-talk. Popé says we will lose the spirit-ways that are ours, and the young will forget. So he talks and stirs up the young men."

He walked a little way in silence, head down, dejected.

"For many seasons, Popé only counseled against listening to the Spanish medicine men," he continued. "Now, he urges violence."

"But, Uncle, that would only be against the Spanish. Your people and mine are friends."

Blue Corn nodded.

"Yes, but . . . I do not know, Red Feather. They may oppose your trading with the Spanish."

"How could that harm them?"

Blue Corn shrugged.

"In things of the spirit, men do not think clearly."

"But we must trade," Red Feather insisted. "Uncle, this is our biggest train. Sixteen pack horses, heavy packs of prime furs and robes, ours and the Head Splitters'. There is nothing else to do with them. And we need the metal tools."

Blue Corn was silent a little longer, but finally answered.

"You do what you must. But, my son, I fear these times are evil. It is past the fork in the path where our people can say 'no, we do not want your medicine.' Blood has been shed."

"Yes, tell me of that."

"I do not know. We hear things. Since the Spanish killed our Elders, there is much hate. The Spanish patrols do not come out this far anymore. They are afraid. An arrow from the darkness . . . then they catch and kill one of our people. The wrong one, of course, and this calls for vengeance. It is bad."

Red Feather had not realized that the situation had deteriorated this far.

"But still, Uncle, we are friends of both sides. Surely, this is not our fight, and we are in no danger. We deal with the trader and with the soldiers, not the medicine men. We will go to Santa Fe, do our trading, and leave quickly."

"Do what you must," Blue Corn said again, unconvinced. "But remember, my son, when dogs fight, anyone interfering may be bitten."

"I do not wish to interfere, Uncle. This is their argument, not ours."

Blue Corn did not answer. He had stated his position, and obviously saw no need to continue the conversation.

Another thought struck Red Feather.

"Uncle, how is it that your pueblo has escaped this?"

Blue Corn sighed.

"We have tried to do as they wish. Their priests come and tell their stories, and we listen. We do our sacred songs and dances only in secret. But now, this enrages those who follow Popé. He wants us to resist, to refuse to listen to the Spanish medicine men. But if we do, then the Spanish soldiers beat or kill us."

Red Feather slowly began to understand the precarious position of Blue Corn's village.

"Uncle," he said quietly, "you are right. These are evil times."

3

» » »

One moment the sandy slope was empty, with no living thing in sight, except a distant eagle drawing his circles in the blue of the mountain sky. The next, it was populated by heavily armed men. There were at least twenty of them, carrying bows, a few with spears, and all wearing knives at their waists. They had seemed to sprout magically from behind the red-brown rocks, from the silvery greasewood which straggled along the slope, and even from the soil itself.

Red Feather tried to appear calm as he reined in his horse. This encounter was a total surprise, though it should have been expected, he told himself irritably. He looked back along the wavering line of pack animals. The other men were reacting calmly, as he would expect. Long generations of confrontation on the prairie had established custom in such a meeting. They would wait while the leaders met and talked, and then act according to how that conversation developed.

A tall young man, flanked by two companions, now strode confidently down the slope toward Red Feather's horse. The others waited, weapons ready. Red

Feather was irritated, partly at himself. He should have had outriders scouting ahead and to the sides. The People called them "wolves," these scouts who circled the main column like wolves circling a moving herd of buffalo. Yes, he should have had wolves out.

The young leader of the strangers was dressed in the loose tunic and leggings of the pueblo people. Good, thought Red Feather. At least, I know their customs.

"Who are you? Where are you going?" barked the young man in Spanish.

Red Feather's anger flared, and he made a concerted effort to calm himself before he answered. This abrupt demand was quite impolite and demeaning. In addition, there was an implied insult in the man's choice of Spanish to address strangers. These were, in all likelihood, some of the revolutionaries led by Popé. That he would address strangers in Spanish implied that they were already considered enemies. Red Feather recalled that Popé himself was said to refuse the use of the Spanish tongue, though he understood it fluently.

Red Feather drew himself up tall in the saddle and tried to appear as dignified as possible.

"I am Red Feather, of a tribe far to the east," he said calmly.

He used the language of his wife's pueblo people. This would, hopefully at least, strengthen the idea that they were friends, if not allies. The other man seemed startled for a moment, then quickly recovered his composure.

"How is it that you speak our tongue?" he asked, in a slightly less abrasive tone.

"It is my wife's language," Red Feather replied stiffly. "Her father's name is Blue Corn."

"Ah, yes," nodded the young man. "I know of him.

A good man, it is said, though he deals with the Spanish."

A look of realization crossed the dark face, and he glanced at the pack horses.

"What is in your packs?" he demanded suspiciously. "Supplies for the Spanish?"

"Of course not!" Red Feather snapped. "We have furs and robes, to trade for the things we need. Metal knives, arrow points, spearheads."

For the first time, a broad smile lit the face of the other man.

"Weapons!" he chortled. "Good! We can use more weapons."

Red Feather, seething inwardly, held his temper in check. This was no time to cause an argument by pointing out that the packs, and whatever merchandise might result from their trade, were the property of the People and their allies the Head Splitters. Certainly, he had no intention of turning the proceeds over to some roving band of fanatics. But it seemed prudent to keep such thoughts quiet for the present. He was thinking rapidly ahead. After they finished trading, perhaps they could return by another route.

"Where is your wife?" the other man asked suddenly.

This revolutionary was no fool, Red Feather realized. The man had been following the same line of thought.

"At the lodge of her father, Blue Corn," Red Feather admitted. "She visits there while we trade."

There seemed no point in lying. If he wished, this young man could quickly verify anything that Red Feather might say. He might as well speak truth.

"Good!" the young man exclaimed cheerfully. "We will wait there for you!"

Again, Red Feather burned with anger. This stranger was assuming that they would gladly turn over all they possessed to the revolutionaries. This was not the way of the People, and sooner or later, this young man would learn it. But not now. They would try to appear cooperative. There would be time to devise a plan. Start home by another way, perhaps, and then return for Moonflower. Ah, well, it would work out.

Red Feather nodded, noncommittally, and gathered his reins.

"We have far to travel," he observed. "Let us be on the trail."

The other man nodded agreement.

"We will be watching," he advised, as if to forestall any tricks.

Red Feather kneed the horse forward. An armed man stood directly in the trail, and for a moment it appeared that he would not quit his position. Then, at the last instant, the warrior seemed to glance at his leader and receive some sort of signal. Quickly, he stepped aside and the train began to file past him. Red Feather felt some sense of relief, but was tense until the last of the pack horses had passed that point. He was still angry over the presumptive arrogance of the men who had stopped them.

He looked back, and saw to his surprise that the revolutionaries had disappeared. The trail, the sandy slope, the hills beyond, were again vacant of any human life.

Turkey Foot now rode forward to join him.

"What is it?" he asked seriously.

"Those are the men Blue Corn spoke of," Red Feather explained. "They hate the Spanish."

Turkey Foot nodded agreeably.

"This is understandable. What did they want with us?"

"It is very confusing, my friend. They want us to hate the Spanish, too, maybe. There is much that I do not understand."

As they rode on, Red Feather told in some detail of his conversation with Blue Corn, and of the desire of the young man to acquire the tools and weapons for which they would trade.

"No!" exclaimed the Head Splitter. "These furs belong to us. We fight, yes?"

Red Feather exhaled a deep sigh.

"It is not so simple. These are my wife's people. If we fight them, they may take vengeance on Blue Corn after we are gone."

Turkey Foot nodded again.

"Then we do not fight them. We only say, 'These things are ours.'"

"I am not sure they will understand, Turkey Foot."

"Cannot our friends, the Spanish, help? We have traded here for many seasons."

"I think not. The Spanish are hard put to defend themselves."

Turkey Foot's eyes grew round.

"*Aiee!* This is big, then!"

"Yes, it seems so."

Turkey Foot shrugged.

"Well, we will see. First, we go to Santa Fe to trade."

4

» » »

The difference in Santa Fe was apparent when they rode into the outskirts of the town. There was an air of tension, an indefinable feeling that reached out to touch and hold, to weigh on the spirit. There was no difference in appearance. Chickens clucked and scratched in the dust, pigs lay in the shade in make-shift pens. Yet, was it just a feeling, that sense of appre-hension or fear on the faces that looked out onto the street?

Red Feather shrugged it off. He had merely been deeply affected, he decided, by the events of the past few days. The conversation with Blue Corn had unset-tled him, but even more, there had been the encounter on the trail. Only then did the thought really begin to sink home. A bad situation did exist, and he and his family were part of it, along with the others who formed the pack train.

He looked over his shoulder at White Fox. The boy was sitting tall, trying to appear experienced and adult. Red Feather had been about that age himself, he re-called, on his first pack trip. He could relate to White Fox's feelings right now. To some extent, he regretted bringing the boy. He had not realized the danger, the unrest in this part of New Spain.

He smiled to himself. The worst he could imagine could be no worse for White Fox than his own first trip. His blundering encounter with the French exploring party, the ensuing misunderstanding in which he had been wounded. . . . *Aiee*, it could be no worse for White Fox, no matter what happened. No, the boy must grow up, must learn to meet the world in his own turn, to make his mistakes as his father had, and his father before him.

The sense of apprehension was still strong as they turned into the street where Gutierrez, the trader, held forth. Red Feather felt better. Now they would be secure. They could rid themselves of their packs and the resulting responsibility, camp overnight, and then leave quickly with their trade goods.

He was planning how, while Turkey Foot and the others began the trading, he would take White Fox and pay a courtesy visit to Captain Díaz. It would please him to do so, and Díaz would be pleased to meet the grandson of his friend Woodchuck. But first they must unload, and bring the packs inside. He glanced at the sky to see how much daylight remained. Yes, it was going well.

They drew rein in front of Gutierrez' store and the proprietor looked out. There was a strange look on his face for an instant, a mixture of surprise and concern. It was there for only an instant. Then it dissolved into the usual broad grin that split the leathery countenance to expose snow-white teeth and crinkle his eyes to mere slits.

"Buenos días, amigo!" he called, stepping outside to

stand under the overhanging shade of the portico. "I had not expected you!"

"Why not, my friend?" Red Feather responded, swinging down from his horse. "We always come at this time."

"Yes, but . . ." Gutierrez glanced furtively up and down the street. "There is trouble, Red Feather."

Red Feather now saw that the trader looked old and tired and frightened. There was much more silver in his hair than there had been only a year ago. The man had aged more in the past season than in all the years Red Feather had known him.

Again there flashed through Red Feather's mind the odd behavior they had encountered. Since Raton Pass, everyone he had seen was acting strangely. Blue Corn and his people, then the band of revolutionaries on the mountain trail. Now, Gutierrez. Everyone in the entire area seemed to feel the threat of impending events He must talk with Gutierrez later. The trader would give him a more realistic view of the situation in Santa Fe.

But for now, they must unload. Lashings were loosened, and men began to carry the heavy packs inside. Gutierrez stooped over a bundle, cut the tie, and riffled through the otter skins.

"These are prime quality, Red Feather. Some of your best." He stood, and shrugged in a display of futility. "But they are not worth much."

For a moment, Red Feather thought that this was the overture to bargaining. Gutierrez had always taken a certain amount of delight in the harangue, the give and take. In the end he had always been fair and honest through the years, but the joy for the trader was in the trading. This time there was no joy, no anticipation, only the tired resignation.

"What is it, my friend?" Red Feather asked.

The trader spread his palms to indicate his helplessness.

"Times are bad. Supplies are slow to arrive from Mexico. There is little food."

"But your people raise food here."

"Not enough. We have always traded with the natives . . . the pueblo people, you know. But now, there is little trade."

"Why not?"

"There are many of us, so more food is needed. But mostly, the natives do not wish to trade."

He paused, looked around the store, and then motioned as he turned to the door.

"Come outside."

He led the way to the street, out of earshot of the others, and turned to face Red Feather.

"My friend," Gutierrez said seriously, "you know the padres wish the natives to give up their dances and superstition."

Red Feather was a bit slow in answering. As long as he had known Gutierrez, he had felt that here was a man of understanding. The trader made no trouble for anyone, and was respected by all. Yet here was evidence that even Gutierrez did not understand the religion of the kivas, and its importance to the growing of the corn. It was pressure from the Spanish missionaries that had ultimately caused the Elders to protest, and Popé to react to their imprisonment with militant zeal.

Gutierrez hurried on.

"Now the padres are *demanding* loyalty to Christ, but there are some of the natives who refuse."

Red Feather nodded, well aware of that side.

"So," Gutierrez continued, "things become worse. We get fewer supplies from Mexico, the natives will not trade us food. . . . I think they are hiding it . . . and the padres want the soldiers to punish them. The patrols are attacked by the rebels, who fade into the mountains. . . . Mother of God, my friend, it is bad."

He shook his head sadly, then looked up, apologetic.

"But forgive me. I am impolite. How is your family? Woodchuck, your father? And what of Sky-Eyes and Pale Star? Ah, that woman is a trader!" he chuckled.

"All well," Red Feather smiled. "I will take your greeting. My wife is with her people until we return."

"Good," nodded Gutierrez. "She will be safe there."

It was an odd remark, one more evidence of this attitude of impending doom.

"Our youngest son is here," Red Feather pointed. "The young man with the pack, there."

Gutierrez chuckled.

"He looks much as you did on your first trip. What were you called? Ah, yes, Ground Squirrel, the Little Woodchuck."

Red Feather smiled, a little ruefully. He had outgrown the childhood name during that summer, and taken the name of his grandfather, chief of the Eastern band.

"This boy is called White Fox," Red Feather explained. "Come and meet him, and then I want to take him to meet Díaz."

"Ah, Díaz is gone," Gutierrez said sadly. "Of course. You did not know."

"Gone?"

"Yes, back to Spain. There has been much change. New assignments, more changes."

"Then who is chief of the soldiers?"

Gutierrez spread his palms in his characteristic gesture of helpless frustration.

"Who knows? The changes are fast, now. If the padres think the soldiers are not doing enough to bring the natives into line, they complain to the governor. Then there is another change."

"But we must make a courtesy visit."

Gutierrez pondered a moment.

"Maybe not. It would have no useful purpose."

"But is there no one? One we know?"

"I think not, Red Feather. Many have been sent elsewhere. Let me think on this. Come, we will trade, camp tonight, and we will talk of this again before you leave."

5

» » »

In later days, Red Feather was to regret many times over that he had not taken the trader's advice. Even with the inescapable feeling that something was terribly wrong, it was hard to accept the warning.

"You should finish the trading quickly and leave," Gutierrez had advised after much consideration. "The trouble is here. Take your people far away."

But the sense of propriety, of etiquette, would not allow Red Feather to do so. Among the people of the plains, custom decreed that visitors pay a courtesy call on the chief. Since his first trip to Santa Fe with his father and Sky-Eyes, they had always paid the formal call on Captain Díaz. Now even though Díaz was gone, the duty visit seemed inescapable.

"It will not be long," he assured Gutierrez. "We will return by dark. You and Turkey Foot go ahead with the trading."

He turned to his son.

"Come, Fox. We will make the duty visit."

By the time they had arrived in the plaza, shadows were lengthening, and Red Feather was becoming uneasy. Heavily armed soldiers walked the streets, always in pairs. He recognized none of the soldiers, and they cast suspicious glances as the two from the prairie passed. Red Feather was considering a hasty retreat, but it might easily attract even more unwelcome attention.

He led the way across the square and approached the portico along the front of the building. White Fox was staring in amazement at the size of the structure. Red Feather smiled to himself at the wonder in the boy's eyes, and again recalled his own first visit here with his father.

His thoughts were brought suddenly back to the present by a burly soldier in blue who blocked the steps, his lance at the ready.

"Halt!" the corporal demanded in Spanish. "No one goes in here. What is your business?"

"We are traders," Red Feather explained politely, "friends of your Captain Díaz. I have heard . . ."

"Friends of Díaz?" the soldier sneered. "He is gone."

He appeared more suspicious than ever.

"So we have heard," Red Feather acknowledged. "But I would speak with your new captain."

"What is your purpose?"

Red Feather spread his hands placatingly.

"Only to show our respect. We have brought him a small gift."

He drew out an otter skin and held it up. "Oiling the palm," Sky-Eyes called such gifts when they were given to the Spanish with whom the People dealt. The soldier reached suddenly and seized the fur. It was an impolite thing to do, but Red Feather allowed it to happen, not willing to challenge the sentry in so tense a situation.

"It is for your captain," he protested mildly.

"I will give it to him. Now, move along."

Anger flared in Red Feather. The soldier would keep the valuable fur, and say nothing to his superiors.

"Good. We will wait to see him," Red Feather stated firmly.

There was a chuckle of amusement from a second soldier who had been standing in the shadows of the doorway. He now stepped into the open on the portico. On his sleeve were the stripes which signified the rank of sergeant. Red Feather had long ago learned to distinguish between such sub-chiefs.

The newcomer swaggered out to the steps, and casually looked at the otter skin in the corporal's hand. He stroked the silken fur with a thumb.

"You are traders? You have more like this?"

"Yes, señor. These and others. We have traded here for many seasons."

"Where are your packs?"

There was a small cry of warning in the back of Red Feather's mind, but he might as well be truthful. Anything he said could be easily verified.

"At the store of the trader, Gutierrez," he said.

The swarthy sergeant nodded.

"Come inside," he beckoned.

Red Feather and White Fox mounted the steps and followed the sergeant, who now carried the gift otter skin. He walked down the hall to the door that Red Feather knew led to the captain's office, and beckoned them inside. Yet another stranger sat at the clerk's desk in the outer office. Gutierrez was certainly right. There had been many changes. White Fox looked apprehensively around the room, a little like a trapped animal. His father was sympathetic. He had the same dread of closed places himself. It was foreign to the spirit of the People, nomads of the open plain.

The sergeant stepped into the inner office for a moment, then beckoned to them from that doorway. A fat, soft-looking officer sat behind the desk, stroking the otter skin. He looked up, a bored expression on his face.

"You wish to trade this?" he asked.

"No, señor, that is a gift for you. We trade other furs at the store of Enrico Gutierrez."

The fat captain nodded. There was something ominous about his apparent carelessness and disinterest.

"For what do you trade?"

"Knives, señor. Arrow points. Tools of metal."

Now the piggy little eyes of the captain narrowed to slits.

"Yes," he hissed. "Weapons!"

"No, no, Señor Captain. My people are buffalo hunters, far away on the plains. We need these things to hunt. Did not Captain Díaz tell you of our trading here? We have done so for many seasons."

"Díaz!" the captain snorted. "The traitor! Yes, I might have known. He had a reputation for softness with savages."

The man said "savages" as if it were an oath, a dirty word that soiled the mouth. Red Feather heard the shuffling of feet in the outer office. It was tempting to turn and look to see what the clerk was doing, but his attention was riveted on the captain's face, now reddening with anger.

"You have come to buy arms!" the captain almost shouted in accusation.

"No, señor," Red Feather protested. "We have always . . ."

"Silence, dog!" The voice of the sergeant roared in interruption.

Almost simultaneously a heavy blow struck the back of Red Feather's neck, and he fell to his knees, half senseless. He was dimly aware that there were more soldiers rushing into the room. He saw White Fox turn to fight, and go down under a wave of blue uniforms.

By the time his sensibilities began to return, both of them were trussed firmly. Someone hauled him roughly to his feet to stand again before the desk of the captain. He glanced around the room. White Fox looked frightened, and a trickle of blood ran down his right cheek from a cut over the eye. Otherwise, the boy appeared uninjured.

From the shadows behind them stepped an older man in the plain robe of the Spanish medicine man. The newcomer looked the captives over curiously.

"Good work, Captain," he congratulated. "We will put a stop to these devil-worshiping heathen and their rebellion."

"Thank you, padre," the captain smiled smugly. "Only my duty."

"Señor, this is a mistake," Red Feather began.

"Silence, heathen," snapped the priest. "The mistake is yours."

Then his face softened as he looked at White Fox. He shook his head sadly.

"So young," he said sympathetically. "Well, fear not, young man. You will have a chance to repent and accept Christ before we hang you."

He turned and left the room.

"Take them away," sneered the fat captain, stroking the shiny fur of his otter skin.

6

》》》

Red Feather sat on the dirt floor of the cell with his back propped against the wall. It was not yet completely dark outside. Through the barred window he could still see an orange glow near the earth's rim, as the rest of the sky faded to the dark purple of night. The back of his head throbbed from the effects of the blow that had knocked him to his knees. He still resented that bitterly. It had been unnecessary. He did not know whether he had been struck with a club or weapon of some kind, or merely with a fist.

Ah, it was no matter. His main concern was for White Fox. *Aiee*, why had he ever chosen to bring the boy? He looked at the form of his son, curled against the wall. Except for the cut over his right eye, Fox was uninjured. With the resiliency of youth, he had curled up to sleep while the opportunity offered. Red Feather envied his son this luxury. He could not possibly sleep, but was glad for White Fox's ability to do so.

Of course, the boy did not understand the significance of the priest's remark about hanging. Red Feather doubted that he was even aware of such a death. Punishment was rare among the People, because it was rarely necessary. Extreme punishment might include banishment from the tribe, but even this had not occurred during the lifetime of White Fox.

The boy was also unaware of the thing Blue Corn had mentioned, the trapping of the spirit by not allowing it to escape as the rope tightened around the throat. Red Feather raised a hand to feel his own neck. What would it feel like? He tried to imagine how a spirit would feel, trapped in a dying body. He shuddered in the growing darkness. He wondered if it was actually true, the trapped spirit Blue Corn had told of. Surely, as the flesh fell away from the bones in the process of decay, there would appear holes through which to escape. Or would the soul die before such an opportunity offered? He wished he could talk to Prairie Dog, the medicine man. He was wise in such things. Almost as wise, it was said, as his father, Looks Far, the great medicine man who had brought about the alliance with the Head Splitters. Prairie Dog would know about these things of the spirit. But in the present situation, it seemed highly unlikely that he could ever speak to Prairie Dog again. Or anyone else of the People, he thought glumly.

He wondered what the others of the trading party were doing. They would have finished unloading, possibly begun to trade, but the coming of darkness would interrupt the process. It was best not to trade in poor light. Gutierrez liked it no better than the People. So, when darkness came and the two had not returned, Gutierrez would close his store to await the better light of day. Turkey Foot would take the others to the usual campground outside of town to await them there.

No, he thought, that will not be how it is. They would know that something was wrong. Gutierrez would try to use his connections to find out what had happened. He would urge Turkey Foot to take the others away. To Blue Corn's pueblo, even, if it seemed advisable. Turkey Foot, who had known the trader for years, would follow his advice. Later, when the prisoners were released or were able to escape, they could rejoin the others.

Red Feather shifted his back against the wall. He did not really believe it. The situation was far more hopeless than that. How he wished that he had some information. Surely, Gutierrez would find a way to send a message.

In such a situation, the basic approach of the People was extremely helpful. Do not worry, it was always advised, about that which has not happened yet. Let each day have its own sunlight. Sometimes his father and Sky-Eyes, he had noticed, had difficulty in actually living this attitude. They could be impatient. It was their different upbringing, in the far-off tribes of a place called France. But they tried, and at least partially achieved the contentment that was a natural heritage of the People. So, Red Feather did as his mother's people would do. He waited.

"The boy is your son?"

The voice came out of the darkness on the other side of the cell. It was now too dark to see more than dim outlines, but Red Feather realized that the old man had spoken. There were two other prisoners in the cell where they had been unceremoniously thrown. An old man sat against the inside wall and a younger one lounged on the thin litter of straw which was the only furnishing of the room. No one had spoken until now.

The old man had used the tongue of the pueblos, probably to see if the newcomers would understand.

"Yes," Red Feather answered. "My son."

"You are outsiders," the other stated.

It was a question as well as a statement of fact.

"Yes. Traders, from the plains to the east. Our tribe is called Elk-dog People."

"I have heard of this."

There was silence for a little while and then the old man spoke again.

"You speak my tongue well. How is this?"

"My wife is of your people. Moonflower, daughter of Blue Corn."

"Ah, yes, of course! And you are Woodchuck?"

"No. Woodchuck is my father. I am Red Feather."

"Of course. You are too young . . . the seasons pass quickly."

Red Feather was just beginning to realize the meaning of such remarks by the older ones of his own tribe.

"You came to trade?" The old man continued the conversation.

"Yes. We need metal for tools and knives, arrow points. We have done so for many seasons."

"Ah, yes. But now, these are seen as weapons?"

"This is as the soldier chief said," Red Feather agreed.

He would have liked to ask about death by the rope which trapped the spirit, but was reluctant. He did not know this man well enough to talk of such things. He did not wish to show fear.

"What is your offense?" he asked instead.

The old man sighed.

"Teaching the sacred dances and songs."

"You are one of the Elders, then?"

"Yes. I have tried to deal fairly with the Hairfaces, and still teach the young the old ways. They will not have it both ways."

Red Feather thought of Blue Corn, whose attitude was much the same. Would he, too, be in such a danger? The situation looked worse and worse. There was a rustling sound outside the window, and a loud whisper.

"Red Feather?"

Red Feather jumped to his feet.

"Gutierrez?"

"Yes! I did not know if I could find you!"

He spoke in Spanish, his voice tense and anxious.

Red Feather tried to look out through the barred window, but it was too high. He grasped the bars to lift himself up. In this way he could look out, but only for a few moments. He made out the dark bulky shape of the trader, crouched against the outside of the wall. It was apparent that the short, heavy-set Gutierrez would not be able to pull himself up to the window. Red Feather dropped back to the floor.

"Where are the others?" he asked. "What is happening, Enrico?"

The voice of the trader nearly cracked with emotion as he answered.

"Gone!" he choked. "It is bad, my friend. No, do not speak. I must tell you quickly and then go."

For the first time, Red Feather began to see a new side of the situation. Gutierrez, by welcoming his old friends, had put himself at considerable risk. If Díaz had been removed from his command as chief of the soldiers for only being sympathetic . . . *aiee!* Gutierrez was guilty of trading in weapons with a potential enemy. Even now he might be a fugitive. He had taken much risk just to come and inform Red Feather.

But what was happening?

7

» » »

From the time Enrico Gutierrez looked out of his doorway to see his friends from the plains, he knew there was trouble. It was obvious that they did not understand the desperately serious mood of the town. But he could not turn them away after more than twenty years of yearly association. It had been profitable for him, true, but more than that, friendship.

His first contact with these nomads had raised his suspicions. Díaz, then a lieutenant of dragoons, had brought Sky-Eyes and his small party to trade, with the firm suggestion that they be treated as honored visitors. The suggestion had originated, it seemed, higher in the chain of command. Gutierrez was a bit resentful, suspicious, and reluctant at first, feeling that there was an attempt on the part of Díaz and his superiors to take advantage of him. He dared not protest too much, because he had no way of knowing how high in the chain of command the coercion might go.

To his surprise, he found that he related well to the "Elk-dog People." Far from being ignorant savages, these were intelligent and perceptive people. An even greater surprise was that Pale Star, wife of their leader, was an experienced trader. Ah, there was a woman! Not only beautiful, but quick and shrewd, and with a sense of humor. Sky-Eyes, who as it turned out was some sort of renegade Frenchman, spoke not only that language but Spanish, as well as the tongue of his wife's people, and probably a handful of other savage languages.

Gutierrez had liked these people, and had helped them in their effort to acquire iron for arrowheads, and steel knives and lance points. Their trading relationship had ripened into lasting friendship. Now, a generation later, who would have ever suspected that the relationship would become dangerous to both? There were many things that Gutierrez did not understand about the current troubles. It had to do with a continuing push by the padres to Christianize the savages, and the natives' reluctance to give up their superstitions. But he had been in Santa Fe for a long time. Long enough to know that there was more to the ceremonies of the kivas than could be easily understood. The padres called it devil-worship, but Gutierrez could see little evil that had come of it. He had carefully kept these thoughts to himself, kept them even from his wife. If the padres knew . . . Mother of God, he'd be paying penance for the rest of his life. Or worse, even.

To further complicate the whole confused mess, it was his understanding that the ceremonies of the pueblo people were not even similar to those of the people from the plains.

Ah, well, religion was no concern of his. Let others worry about it. The concern for Gutierrez was that it interfered with business. Times were bad, anyway, with changing politics and little support from home for the far-flung colonies of New Spain. Now, the harder the padres tried to teach of the Blessed Virgin, the less cooperation there was from the natives, less food to trade, more ill will.

Of course, the natives of an occupied territory must be shown who rules. Still, a mild-mannered man like Gutierrez recoiled from excessive force. It was more his nature to bargain his way along. The hangings, he thought, were excessive. Even chopping the right hand off that native over in the other town. How in Christ's name, Gutierrez had asked himself, can a man be made more productive by losing a hand?

So, with the situation worsening rapidly, it was with some dread that he viewed the arrival of Red Feather's party. If they had brought food to trade, even, or if they wanted something else. But to bring furs and robes, luxuries, almost, to trade for weapons? By the blood of Christ, it looked bad. He understood it. Díaz would have understood, but Díaz was gone. So was Villa, the old sergeant, and all of those from the earlier days that now appeared so good when one looked back. Gutierrez could think of no one now who could be trusted to understand. The people from the plains simply needed tools to carry out their business of hunting. It had nothing to do with the problems of New Spain.

Gutierrez had tried his best to dissuade Red Feather from going to see the successor of Díaz. But Red Feather was as hidebound to custom as any Spaniard could be. The custom of his people decreed that a courtesy call must be paid by a visitor. They had always done so. That was fine, as long as the "chief" on whom they called was Díaz. But now . . .

Gutierrez had tried to hurry the trading after Red

Feather and his son left the store. However, Turkey Foot, always methodical and thorough, would not be hurried. Gutierrez became more and more concerned and frustrated, which in turn made Turkey Foot suspicious.

When the sound of jingling equipment and many horses' hooves sounded in the street, Gutierrez leaped quickly to the door. A platoon of lancers jogged easily down the street, but their demeanor could not be mistaken. Their purpose appeared centered on the store of Enrico Gutierrez, where the pack animals of the People were still tied in the street. Gutierrez raced back inside, moving faster than he had in years.

"Quick! Out the back door!" he urged.

There was a moment of nonunderstanding, because of the confusion of different languages. Then Turkey Foot realized that the trader was frantic.

"What is it?" he demanded.

"The soldiers come!"

"But they are friends."

"No, no. Not these. Go, now."

Turkey Foot was unconvinced.

"Then we fight, not run."

Mother of God, thought Gutierrez. What can I do?

"It would make trouble for Red Feather!" he blurted desperately. "Please. Go now!"

Turkey Foot nodded. Now there was a reason. He turned and spoke a few short words to the others. Quickly, they slipped through the back door, across the yard, and over the wall.

Gutierrez ran back to the door to see the platoon drawing to a halt. The commander, a stern-looking young lieutenant, glanced over the horses tied at the rail or to nearby trees. Then, to his alarm, Gutierrez noticed that one of the young men of the trading party was standing among the pack horses, curiously watching the soldiers. He had apparently been outside to check on the animals when the others left. Gutierrez would have warned him, but could think of no way to do so.

The lieutenant rode up to the door and dismounted to look inside. Packs of furs were open and in disarray on the floor and the counters.

"Ah," observed the lieutenant, "you are trading with the savages."

"Yes, señor, it is my work, the trading," Gutierrez said respectfully.

"For weapons?" the officer snorted, pointing to a pile of knives and bar iron on a counter.

"Señor, these are not local natives," the trader pleaded. "They are hunters from the far plains. They need . . ."

"Lies!" cried the lieutenant. "One savage is as bad as another."

He turned to two troopers who had followed them inside.

"Arrest this man!"

Then he paused for a moment.

"No, wait."

He turned to Gutierrez.

"I will confiscate these goods and the horses outside, as evidence. Your store is closed, and will be locked at the pleasure of the Crown. Now, where are these savages?"

Gutierrez shrugged.

"I do not know, señor. They fled when your dragoons came."

The officer turned to a trooper.

"There was one outside. Put him in irons. We will question him. Impound the horses."

"Señor," ventured Gutierrez, "it may be that he can tell you nothing. He . . ."

He was about to suggest that the young man probably knew no Spanish, but the lieutenant interrupted. He whirled on the trader.

"We have ways to loosen his tongue," he warned. "You had best mind your own."

There was a scuffle outside, and Gutierrez stepped to the doorway. His worst fears were realized. Young Red Dog, understanding no Spanish at all, only knew that these warriors were attempting to steal the horses. He tried communicating in the tongue of the Head Splitters, that of the People, and in the sign-talk, but could not make himself understood.

Desperately, he reached to his waist for his throwing ax. It had hardly touched his hand, however, when sabers came whispering out of their scabbards. One of the "long knives" flashed in the setting sun and young Red Dog fell, to bleed out his life in the dust of a place many sleeps from home.

The troopers methodically gathered the horses and began to herd them back up the street. The lieutenant assigned two men to guard the store, and then turned to Gutierrez. The trader was still standing awestruck at the killing.

"You, trader," the lieutenant snapped, "you love these savages so much, take care of that dead one."

Gutierrez nodded dumbly. The lieutenant turned his horse to ride away.

"Why did you let him go, Lieutenant?" asked the sergeant at his side. "The man is guilty as sin!"

"Of course," chuckled the officer. "But now, I want

you to pick a pair of smart hombres to follow him. I want to know where he takes that dead savage, and all about everyone he talks to."

Gutierrez carefully approached the body of Red Dog. He did not know what manner of burial this man's customs would prefer. However, it was necessary to straighten the limbs and arrange the corpse before it became stiff. The whole thing was not to his liking. He dreaded touching the cold flesh. Still, aside from the command by the lieutenant, he felt a certain obligation to this companion of his friends.

He managed to straighten the bent knees and extend the body on its back as if in repose. At that point he became quite unnerved by the staring eyes that would see no more. He closed the unresisting lids, only to note with horror that they partly opened again. He thought a moment, and then fished in his pocket for a couple of coins. The silver pesos held the lids closed effectively, though he avoided looking at the face. The grotesque appearance of the blind-staring silver disks was like some bug-eyed creature from a nightmare. It was almost as bad as the open eyelids. The two troopers who had been left as sentries watched him with amusement.

He managed to cross the arms over the chest in a position of repose, but they would not stay. The left hand kept falling away, dropping to the side. Gutierrez solved the problem by loosely tying the wrists with a thong. He could remove it later, after the stiffening had occurred.

Now he spread a buffalo robe on the ground, and dragged the body onto it, puffing a little from exertion and nervousness. He folded the robe around the corpse, tying it in place with thongs. After much soul-searching he retrieved his pesos at the last moment, before covering the face. He dragged the unfortunate Red Dog, in his decently wrapped condition, under the roof of the portico and against the wall of the store.

It was growing quite dark now, and Gutierrez straightened to look up and down the street. He was sweating nervously, despite the chill of the mountain twilight. Now he would try to find what had happened to Red Feather. He shuffled off toward the plaza. Mother of God, he would be glad when this was over. He dreaded what his wife would say. She would likely scold him about becoming involved in things that did not concern him. But he must, at least, find out what had happened to Red Feather.

8

>> >> >>

Red Feather listened at the window while Gutierrez rapidly told of the events at the trader's store.

". . . and they killed one of your young men."

"But why?"

"They were taking the horses. He tried to stop them. The soldiers have seized all your goods, and mine . . . my store . . . they arrested me, but then let me go. I have taken care of your dead one."

The trader was practically in tears.

"Where are the others?" demanded Red Feather.

"I do not know. I got them out the back door before the soldiers came."

"It is good. They will go to the camping place and wait for me. Gutierrez, could you go and tell them? Tell them to go to Blue Corn's village and wait for me there."

"But you are . . ."

"Yes, yes, but they must leave now, get away from Santa Fe. Tell them!"

"*Sí*. I will do this."

He paused a moment, then continued.

"I am sorry, my friend."

"It is not your doing. Now, go! And I thank you for your help. May it be better for you."

Gutierrez' voice was unsteady with emotion as he answered.

"For you, also."

Both men felt the unspoken belief that they would probably never meet again. Red Feather lifted himself by the window bars to watch the heavy shape of the trader shuffle across the street and disappear into the darkness.

White Fox was awake, but had not understood the whispered conversation in Spanish.

"What is it, Father? That was the trader?"

"Yes. They have taken our goods and our horses."

"*Aiee!* Who?"

"The soldiers. They caught the trader, too, but let him go. One of our men was killed by the soldiers."

"Who was it?"

"Gutierrez did not know his name. A young man, he said."

"The others were caught?"

"Oh. No, they went out the back door of the trader's lodge."

"Where will they go?"

"To the camping place, maybe. I have asked Gutierrez to tell them to go on to Blue Corn's pueblo."

The boy was quiet for a little while.

"Father," he said finally, "what will happen to us?"

"I do not know. We will meet that as it comes."

The two settled down to a miserable night in the uncomfortable, smelly cell. Red Feather was certain that he could feel the crawling of insects on his skin. He tried not to think of it, but he knew that such places were usually inhabited by an assortment of small blood-sucking creatures. This was a major reason why the People preferred to avoid the lodges of the Growers in their own country. The Growers' dwellings were permanent, half sunken in the ground for shelter from heat or cold. But there was the ever-present animal smell, like the lodge of a bear or the musty smell of the mouse which has entered stored winter food to build his lodge. This cell had much the same odor, that of human body scents and dried urine. Once again, Red Feather marveled that people could live in such a lodge, and wished for the open breezes of the prairie.

But, he told himself, that was the least of their problems. He did not completely understand what their offense had been, although it apparently was the trading for metal weapons. The threat of the rebellious followers of Popé must indeed be great to concern the Spanish so.

He wondered what would happen when the men of the trading party, now on foot, again encountered the rebels. They surely would encounter them, because the rebels seemed to have wolves everywhere, watching for travelers. There was even the possibility that they would be invited to join the rebels. Turkey Foot understood a little Spanish and a little of the pueblo tongue. They could communicate, even without the hand-sign talk that the plains people found so essential, but which was not used in this area.

Yes, the more he thought, the likelier this seemed. The idea of vengeance would appeal to Turkey Foot and the others. They might not go to Blue Corn's at all, but join the rebels in the mountains. If so, it was indeed a pity that they had not been able to save the weapons from Gutierrez' store.

He thought of Moonflower, and was glad for her safety. She would know that something was wrong. She had always been able to tell when he was in trouble, since their first meeting. It had been her stubborn unwillingness to let his spirit go that had kept him alive until the kiva ceremony which had brought it back.

Someone would tell her of his fate, and that of White Fox. Moonflower would be safe in her parents' lodge. She might even marry again. She was still beautiful, even though nearing the end of the child-bearing years.

Red Feather paused, startled at his own thoughts. He had been thinking in terms of her life without him, and without White Fox. Had he already assumed that they would be killed? He had not actually thought that, but the idea had crept in. He must be careful. It was well known how such thoughts could affect coming events. No, he would concentrate on *when* they would be released, or escape, to join the others. That would keep him alert, to take advantage of whatever chance offered. He felt better.

The old man across the little room was snoring loudly now. Red Feather resolved to talk with him again. He must learn more about the daily routine of their captors. This man would be wise, as one of the Elders of his people. The Elders held an office that had always seemed to Red Feather to be part chief and part medicine man. As they grew better acquainted, he might even venture to ask about the death by the rope. Yes, he would certainly talk more with this man.

As if in answer to his thoughts, the snoring stopped. The old man stirred a little, sat up, and then spoke.

"It was the trader, last night?"

"Yes. The soldiers took our goods and killed one of our young men."

"I heard. The others escaped?"

"Yes."

"Good. Maybe they will join Popé?"

Red Feather was astonished. It had taken him a good part of the night to arrive at that conclusion, and this man had already realized it.

"May they find him quickly," the old man went on, "before the soldiers find them."

That was a risk that Red Feather had not even considered. He had assumed that all the soldiers in New Spain would be unable to track down the party from the plains. Turkey Foot was skilled and devious. Of course he could escape the searchers, once in the open.

Then he realized that Turkey Foot and the others were without horses, while their pursuers would be well mounted. But Gutierrez would have warned them.

The old man was speaking again.

"Have you wondered why they released the trader?"

"What?"

Even as he asked the question, he knew the answer, and cursed his own stupidity. The soldiers had caught Gutierrez red-handed, trading weapons to a supposed enemy. No one would release such a prisoner, but they had done so. There was only one possible purpose. The trader had been released so that he could be watched, in the hope that he would make contact with the rebels.

Instead, the trader had come to the jail cell, and then had gone to make contact with the others who had fled from the trader's store. This would make the soldiers more certain than ever—certain both of Gutierrez' guilt, and that the innocent trading party of the People was, in fact, part of the rebel force of Popé.

Red Feather rose, gripped the iron bars in frustration, and stared out into the starry black sky. Only a few sleeps ago, he had been on top of the world, but now that world was turning to dung beneath him.

9

» » »

After the brief whispered conversation through the jail window, Gutierrez knew what he must do. He walked quickly home. A time or two he thought that he saw furtive figures in the street some distance behind him, but decided that his imagination was working too vigorously.

As he had expected, María met him at the door with a reprimand.

"Where have you been?" she scolded. "It is long past dark, and . . ."

She paused, looking at his stricken face.

"What is it, Enrico?"

The trader looked at her for a moment, longing to pour out his story.

"No," he muttered. "María, the less you know, the better. Get me some food, I have much to do tonight."

He sank wearily into a chair, but was up and restlessly pacing before María had brought his torillas and beans. He went to the little corral behind the house and led the donkey out to hitch it to the two-wheeled cart. Back inside, he wolfed down a little food, and then kissed María.

"I will be gone all night, maybe. I go on an errand of sadness for a friend."

He thought a moment longer.

"María, it is bad. The soldiers have closed the store."

"But, Enrico, why?"

"It is a misunderstanding. Do not worry. I will be back."

He kissed her again, and climbed into the cart. The streets were dark and deserted. Only a sliver of the quarter moon nearing the horizon to the west furnished dim light. He clucked to the burro and they moved through the familiar town, now made different by darkness and tension.

Once again, he thought he saw a brief flash of motion between houses ahead. At another place, the burro stopped dead still and peered into a shadowy corner. Gutierrez whacked him impatiently.

"Come on, Pedro. I have enough troubles already. Do not give me more."

They stopped in front of the store and Gutierrez loaded the buffalo skin-wrapped bundle into the cart. Pedro, catching the scent of blood, laid his ears back and rolled white-rimmed eyes, but stood fast. In a moment they moved on, heading out on the old trail, north and east from town. The houses grew smaller, and fell behind.

Gutierrez was not certain where the camping place might be. It was near the trail, he knew, but distances were deceiving at night. How far out of town? The moon had set, and dim starlight barely made it possible to see the trail. If he could only follow it, he felt that he would come to wherever the trading party was camped. Then he could give them the body that bumped along behind him in the cart. Or, at least, ask what they wanted him to do with it. Mother of God, how had he become involved in such a thing?

Suddenly Pedro snorted and stopped. Gutierrez was about to whack him when a dark form seemed to materialize out of the darker night. Gutierrez gulped and sat peering, trying to see the figure that blocked the trail ahead.

The man stepped forward to stand near the donkey.

"*Ak-koh*, trader."

"Turkey Foot? Is it you?"

Gutierrez nearly wept in relief.

"Tell us, where is Red Feather?" Turkey Foot demanded.

"In jail. He asked me to tell you."

"Jail?"

The conversation was in Spanish, and Turkey Foot's command of the tongue did not include that word. There was a moment's discussion with other figures who came alive out of the dark. He turned back to the trader.

"Jail? Like a trap?"

"Yes," agreed Gutierrez.

It was close enough.

"We must get him out!" Turkey Foot announced.

"No, no. He asked that I find you, tell you not to wait for him. Go on, stop at Blue Corn's pueblo. He will meet you there."

"Maybe so," agreed Turkey Foot doubtfully. "What happened to Red Dog?"

"He is dead. In the cart." He jerked a thumb at the still form behind him.

"We thought so. Gutierrez, why? We are not enemies!"

Gutierrez merely spread his palms helplessly.

"Who knows? These are strange times."

"Very strange," agreed Turkey Foot. "Come, camp with us, while we make plans. You have eaten?"

"Yes."

"It is good. Oh yes, trader, the two who followed you . . . do not worry. They have been silenced."

Gutierrez felt the hairs prickle on his neck. He had not even known he was followed. But now . . . These people, his friends, in trying to help him, may have done irreparable damage. They had killed two Spaniards who had apparently been assigned to follow him. When this was discovered, he would be arrested, possibly even charged with murder. A cold sweat broke out on his face. He crossed himself, and murmured a quick prayer to the Blessed Virgin, with whom he was actually only very slightly acquainted.

"What did you say, *amigo?*" asked Turkey Foot.

"Nothing. It was nothing," the trader assured him.

They had only been trying to help him, he knew. But, Mother of God, what could he do now? Maybe he could go back and throw himself on the mercy of the tribunal. Maybe he could explain.

"Come," said Turkey Foot, taking Pedro by the bridle and turning him off the path. "We will plan. If we are to travel, we need horses. We need to bury Red Dog. We can mourn him later. Señor, will you come with us to Blue Corn's lodge, or go back?"

Gutierrez thought rapidly. It certainly looked safer to accompany these men. What a terrible choice. Maybe he would be able to think better in the morning.

"I do not know yet," he said thoughtfully.

Turkey Foot nodded, understanding. They had arrived at the camp, a dark fireless camp. Men were rising from positions of repose to see what the watch of the trail had produced. The entire party gathered around the cart while Turkey Foot spoke briefly in his own tongue, apparently telling the others of Red Feather's plight and of the fate of Red Dog. There was a murmur around the circle.

Then Turkey Foot turned to Gutierrez.

"Now, tell us, señor, where will they have our horses?"

Gutierrez felt that whatever control he had ever had over his life was slipping away.

"I can show you," he said huskily.

10

》 》 》

"**T**here," Gutierrez pointed. "In behind that wall."

It was a large enclosure, surrounded by a thick adobe wall, as high as a man's head. A sentry paced slowly along the outside and around the corner. Two men sprinted forward, and one leaped to the other's shoulders for a moment to look inside. They were back before the sentry reappeared.

"Many horses. More than ours."

"It is good," observed Turkey Foot. "We do not leave empty. We take them all."

There was a quiet chuckle around the group.

"Only two wolves?"

Several men nodded.

"I take one, Otter, can you get the other?"

Black Otter nodded.

"Bull's Horn, you open the door to get the horses out."

Turkey Foot turned to look at Gutierrez, who had not understood a word of the proposed plans.

"*Amigo*, you wait for us, there." He spoke in Spanish, pointing to a tree outlined against the sky a little distance from town. "By the tree."

Gutierrez was relieved. He now viewed this entire incredible adventure with mixed emotions. There had been a time a little earlier when he was almost enthusiastic about the horse-stealing raid. He was bitter and resentful of the high-handed way in which the soldiers had taken over his property. He also felt regret for Red Feather's imprisonment, and sympathy toward the others. Especially, he had bad feelings about the useless killing. At the height of all this resentment, he had volunteered to show them the corral where the horses were kept.

Now, he was beginning to have doubts. When it came to the actual carrying out of the plan to steal the horses, his resolve had weakened. An hour ago, his heart pumping with excitement, he had imagined himself boldly assisting in the recovery of the property of his friends. In the darkness outside the corrals, he shivered as he considered the gravity of this move. He was certain about the brief conversation between Turkey Foot and the others, though he had not understood the words. They were planning to kill the sentries.

Well, what had he expected? Such was the way of life among these people. His shock and surprise, he realized as he shuffled toward the tree on the hill, was at himself. Here he was, a quiet businessman, middle-aged and long established in the town. Well, even a little past middle age, perhaps. He had become soft from physical inactivity, and fat from indulgence. These things became apparent when he tried to exert himself. Even now, climbing the slope toward the tree, he was puffing and wheezing a little. How in Christ's name had he imagined himself performing heroic deeds to recover the property of his friends?

He reached the tree and sank to a sitting position to rest. His rest was short-lived, however. From the area of the corrals came the sound of shuffling hooves. The horses were milling excitedly. Now there was a shout of alarm, and a general sense of seething motion. A musket boomed, and then another, and a horse cried out in fear or pain.

There was a growing thunder of hoofbeats as the horses swept up the hill toward him. Gutierrez rose to his feet, frightened at the herd's approach, wondering if he should run. He compromised by placing himself behind the inadequate protection of the tree as the running animals began to sweep past on both sides. Dust rose to blur the vision and choke the lungs. He began to realize that these were not merely the horses which had been confiscated. Mother of God, this must be all the horses in New Spain.

The thunder began to diminish, and he blinked the dust from his eyes. Some of the horses now approaching carried riders. They were laughing and joking excitedly, and he recognized some of them. There was Black Otter, and yes, Turkey Foot, who reined over toward the tree. He was leading a horse.

"Here, *amigo*, one for you!"

He handed a rawhide rein to Gutierrez. For a moment the trader wondered if he could swing up, but quickly decided that he must. There were sounds of shouts and running feet below. He led the animal close to a boulder, stepped up and swung a leg over. Turkey Foot had already started on. The horse turned to follow the others, so suddenly that Gutierrez was almost unseated, but he grabbed a handful of the mane and hung on, as the horse trotted ahead.

The sounds of pursuit faded behind them, and the pace began to slow. Gutierrez was excited again, exhilarated by the adventure. He had actually taken part in a raid to recover confiscated horses. Here he was, Enrico Gutierrez, riding into the mountains with a band of savages who had just carried out a successful operation against the military garrison at Santa Fe. They had recovered not only their own animals but had stolen most of the other horses at the post.

But then the seriousness of the raid began to sink home to him. He had committed a major crime, had participated in stealing property of the Crown. Worse, they would be pursued. Eventually, there would be a confrontation, perhaps a bloody fight. What would he do then? Could he fight against his own countrymen? Could he fight against anyone? There was no way that he could now remain neutral.

They arrived back at the campground, picked up what few belongings they still possessed, and prepared to move on. A couple of the young men were circling the horse herd, holding them together. Some of the others sorted out their own mounts or picked a better animal for replacement in the gray light of dawn.

Turkey Foot approached Gutierrez.

"We will move on soon," he said. "Our hearts are good for your help. You will tell Red Feather?"

Gutierrez did not answer for a moment. Obviously, Turkey Foot did not understand his position.

"Maybe we can come back to help him," Turkey Foot continued. "Tell him that."

Gutierrez nodded, confused. They were assuming

that he would go back, that for him things would be as
before.

He looked at his donkey cart, partly hidden in the
rocky draw. Just beyond, old Pedro browsed content-
edly, picketed to a bush. Farther up the draw was the
final resting place of Red Dog. Gutierrez had helped to
carry rocks to conceal the grave.

How very much had happened since the last sunrise
over these mountains. It could never be the same
again. This was what Turkey Foot did not realize. Basically, the trader no longer had any choice at all. He
was afraid, deathly afraid, of the uncertainties ahead.
However, he was even more afraid of the certainties
behind. The authorities had already been suspicious of
him. They had had him followed. Those who followed
him had been killed, and that fact, when discovered,
would appear to establish his guilt. He was still not
quite ready to concede that he *was* guilty. Guilty of
consorting with enemies of the Crown, of assisting
with the theft . . . He had only been trying to do
what was right, but no one would understand that. No
one in Santa Fe, at least. These people understood, and
were grateful.

"Turkey Foot," he called after the retreating figure,
"take me with you?"

Turkey Foot reined back.

"You are not going home?"

It was too complicated to explain. Hopefully, someday, there might be a way to rejoin his own people,
and that would be good. But for now, Enrico Gutierrez
had run out of choices. He no longer could go back.

"I cannot," he said slowly. "They would kill me."

"Your own people?" Turkey Foot gasped, astonished.

"Yes. I have helped you."

Turkey Foot nodded in at least partial understanding.

"Then come with us."

Gutierrez walked up the draw and released the burro, which ambled off to seek better browse. He turned to see Turkey Foot staring at the cart.

"We make it look better for you," he announced.

Turkey Foot called to a couple of the others, and together they lifted one side of the cart and dumped it over into the draw. As a final gesture, Turkey Foot shot a couple of arrows into the side of the cart.

"We could kill the long-ears," he suggested.

"No," said Gutierrez quickly. "This is enough."

It pleased him to think of the confusion as the soldiers tried to decipher the puzzling bits of evidence that they would find.

By the time the sun was fully above the horizon, they were moving rapidly along the trail, driving the stolen horse herd.

11
» » »

Red Feather had much time to think in the next few days. There was little else to do in the cramped confines of the cell. Sometimes he tried to watch the square patch of sunlight, divided by the shadow of iron bars. He knew that it moved, because it crept down one wall, across the floor during the course of the day, and a little way up the opposite wall. Then turning red-orange, it would suddenly dissolve into darkness. Though he tried repeatedly, he could never quite *see* the motion, but a little later, could verify that it had taken place.

It was a thing about which to wonder. A better thing, apparently, than their predicament. There seemed to be no answer to that. On the day after their arrest, Red Feather was taken from the cell and led to another room for questioning. The same medicine man he had seen in the captain's office came, and talked a lot, and accused him of misdeeds he did not understand. There seemed to be two separate problems. One was the suspicion of buying weapons to make war on the Spanish. The other was more poorly defined. Somehow it had to do with having a different creation story, and not believing that of this medicine man. Red Feather's Spanish was not the best, but he understood conversation. What he did not understand was the repeated use of the words and phrases which seemed to make little sense. There were suggestions that believing this man's story would somehow preserve one's spirit. Red Feather thought this odd, coming from people who did things like the death by the rope, which was thought to trap the spirit.

Actually, he thought that the creation story as set forth by this medicine man was a good one. He had heard it before. Pale Star, a favorite storyteller of the People, had used it frequently, having learned it long ago. Red Feather enjoyed the rising of First Man from the dust, and the creation of First Woman from one of his ribs. The evil real-snake, influencing the woman, was a nice touch. Yes, a good story. He could truthfully say that he believed it. It was every bit as fine a beginning as that of the People, who had crawled from inside the earth through a hollow cottonwood log. Or the story of the First Four Brothers, who came up out of a lake to establish the Head Splitter nation. That was a good one. Pale Star knew several more, and could make the story of each tribe come alive.

Red Feather did not understand *why* it was so important to the Spanish medicine men to listen to no story but theirs. Were they afraid that the stories of the Elk-dog People, or the pueblos, or the Head Splitters might be considered more enjoyable? *Aiee*, they must lack much confidence in their own stories. He also did not understand the significance of the story of the young medicine man who seemed a great teacher, but was tortured and killed by his own people, only to rise from the dead. It, too, was a good story. But why would anyone want to force people to believe *only* one story? He would ask Prairie Dog. If, of course, he ever saw Prairie Dog again.

If, Red Feather reasoned, he agreed, and truthfully so, that their story was a good one and that he believed it, that should settle that problem. That left only the other matter, that of the weapons. Repeatedly, he told them, these were not to fight the Spanish, not to fight anyone. They were to hunt buffalo. Maybe to trade with people farther east. He did not think that they believed him.

"You buy these things for Popé, the devil-worshiper," the priest accused.

"No!" Red Feather insisted. "But, *señor,* I know of this man. I saw him once, many summers ago. He helped to heal me when I was hurt. But never since."

"Aha! You *do* know him. He has worked his evil spells on you!"

Red Feather was at a loss to understand how healing was evil, but did not answer. He had said too much already.

The soldiers who brought him to this questioning were rough and brutal, but careless. There were two of them. He could have easily killed them and escaped, he thought, but he had young White Fox to think of.

Despite the broad threat which the priest had made at the time of their capture, no one had even questioned the boy. Fox was impatient, of course. After the first night's sleep, he had been ready for anything. Anything, that is, except nothing. He tried his best, but it was obvious that the forced inactivity was very difficult. Once Red Feather reminded him not to wish for something to happen. Eventually something would, and when it did, there was every reason to believe it might be quite unpleasant.

Red Feather had noted that there were other prisoners. When he was taken for questioning his captors led him past other doors of heavy planks, bound with iron, and with small barred openings. At one such opening he caught a glimpse of a dark face with sunken eyes and a look of hopeless resignation. There had been no opportunity to speak or even acknowledge the other's presence. The soldier had shoved him roughly forward at that moment, and he saw the face in the door opening withdraw in alarm.

They were fed once daily, a thin mush that appeared to be of ground corn. Sometimes it contained unidentified dark lumps which the prisoners hoped were beans. In the dim light of the cell, identification was difficult. In no time at all they felt starved for meat. Red Feather would have night-visions of browning hump ribs over a fire of buffalo chips, and awake with hunger pangs. It was a good sign, this vision, lending hope for the future, when it would happen in reality.

On the third day, the old man was taken from the cell. He turned at the door and murmured a few brief words, as the guards urged him forward.

"May it go well with you," he said simply to the other occupants of the cell.

"And you, Uncle," Red Feather answered politely, with the term of respect.

There was a finality about the brief exchange, which would cause Red Feather to think about it for a long time. He initially assumed that the time had come for the old man's release. After all, they had released even Popé himself. But as he thought, the short farewell seemed to carry a more subtle meaning. Yes, the resignation, almost a sadness, on the wrinkled old face carried another message, Red Feather feared. He regretted that he had not taken an opportunity to talk with the man about the rope-death. That still concerned him.

When the old man did not return, it was no surprise. They still did not know whether that marked freedom or death for their recent companion. Red Feather tried to engage the other, the younger prisoner, in talk, but failed. The man only stared silently with large dark eyes. It was impossible to tell whether he understood the attempts at all. He might speak one of the other pueblo tongues, or be unable to hear or to speak. Possibly, he might simply mistrust the strangers. Red Feather tried to recall whether they had heard him speak at all. The old man had spoken briefly to him sometimes, but neither Red Feather nor White Fox could remember whether he had answered. After a day or two, they gave up the effort. They continued to speak to him, but expected no reply.

None of them ever saw the old man again.

It was several days later that White Fox made his discovery. It was quite by accident. He had developed the habit of pulling himself up to the window by grasping the iron bars. He would hang there as long as possible, watching the street, out of pure boredom. Red Feather paid little attention to the activity. It was good for the boy to be occupied in some way.

Darkness was near, and White Fox was watching the sunset, his face pressed against the bars. Red Feather sat on the floor, becoming more depressed. Another sun had come and gone, and there had been no change in their situation. He tried to count on his fingers how many days they had been here. He was wondering why there was no further word from Gutierrez.

The soft pattering sound escaped his attention at first. It was very slight. It seemed to come from beneath the window, where White Fox was dangling. Fox shifted his hold and the sound increased for a moment, then ceased.

Now Red Feather leaned toward that sound.

"Move again, Fox," he whispered.

Yes, there it was again, when White Fox shifted his weight. Red Feather extended an exploring hand in the near darkness along the floor. There was an almost imperceptible sensation of dust or debris striking the back of his hand. The slight sound of the same material pattering on the straw of the floor had caught his attention. He rose quickly to search for its source.

"What is it, Father?" White Fox wondered, dropping to the floor.

Red Feather was grasping the bars, testing each one. Ah, yes, the one on the right! It moved a trifle, and again he felt the dusty trickle on the back of his hand.

"The bar is loose!" he whispered softly.

"Yes, that one is," the puzzled boy responded. "But it is set in holes in the wood."

Red Feather did not answer. He was busily occupied. It was almost completely dark, but there was much that he could tell by feel. The bar rotated slightly, but more importantly, there was motion up and down. He could lift the bar nearly a finger's width before it struck firm resistance at the top. And that in turn, caused more dirt to dribble down on the wooden sill of the window.

He experimented a little longer, and then brushed the windowsill clean. He felt better than he had for several sleeps. Maybe the time *would* come when they could again sit in the open air of the Sacred Hills and smell the odor of browning hump ribs over a fire of buffalo chips.

"Stay away from the window for now," he told White Fox. "When morning comes, we will look at it again."

12

» » »

Enrico Gutierrez bounced along on the back of the stolen horse, every muscle tortured and straining. His left foot was asleep, and try as he would, he was unable to wriggle it enough to rid it of the thousand tiny prickling needles that kept him tense and exhausted. The right foot was little better.

When they stopped at noon, he had slid from the animal to rest and had almost fallen to the ground. His legs were like jelly from the unaccustomed activity. Gutierrez had ridden a horse before, of course, but it had been many years since he had had occasion to do so. And the last time, he had had the advantage of a saddle. How he longed for the comfort of a saddle. Of course, none of the others had a saddle, either. But they were much younger, except for Turkey Foot, who did not really count in such a matter. Turkey Foot was ageless. Old, but tough, wiry, and athletic. How unlike himself, Gutierrez thought ruefully: fat, soft, and short of breath. The man seemed indestructible, jogging ahead there, rounding up strays.

Gutierrez shifted uncomfortably. The backbone of the animal had seemed an advantage at first. It was convenient to grasp, and served to prevent the constant tendency to slide sideways, one way or the other. Now it had become an instrument of torture, knifing up into his crotch. It was worst when he fell behind and the horse was forced to trot to catch up with the others. That uncontrolled bouncing presented a great hazard to his manhood. Once he had descended squarely on an unprotected testicle, forcing an audible grunt of pain from his throat. He felt like he had been kicked in the pit of the stomach. He thought for a moment that he would vomit, and it was all he could do just to hang on. For some time there was total pain, from his lower ribs to below his groin. He was afraid to take a deep breath, because it seemed certain that it would hurt.

Now, that particular injury had subsided to a dull ache. It had been replaced, however, by the cramping in his muscles. Soft and unused, every fiber seemed intent on protesting the indignity of such treatment.

At the rest stop, Gutierrez had actually considered staying behind when the others went on. He did not think he could climb back aboard the four-legged source of his agony. Besides, he was afraid. Ahead in the mountains lay the Unknown. There was no way of even suspecting what hardships he would have to face. He had been an idiot. What had ever possessed him to accompany these men, who, after all, were little more than strangers? Even Turkey Foot, whom he had known for years, he did not really know. Once each year, they met briefly, but this amounted in total to less than a score of meetings. No, he would let them go on, and then make his way back to Santa Fe. He could claim that he had been abducted. All other discrepancies he could talk his way out of. Would not the wrecked cart in the gully support such a story?

In the end, when the time came to move on, Gutierrez led his horse over to a boulder, painfully climbed upon the rock, and remounted. He was afraid of what might lie ahead, to be sure. Yet he was more afraid of going back. No matter how much he might dread the uncertainty, it was a better choice, he concluded, than the certainty that awaited him in Santa Fe. He could not avoid the fact that he had helped the trading party from the plains escape through his back door. And they *had* been in the process of actually trading for weapons. It would not go well with him, in the present atmosphere of distrust.

He was not certain what had caused the growing strain in dealings with the natives. The padres were increasingly rigid, it was true, trying hard to find fault. But was that the result of the activities of the medicine man Popé? There had been rumors of his activities ever since his release from prison last year. Popé was bitter because of the imprisonment, the natives said, but that led again to the reasons for his imprisonment. He had insisted on teaching the old dances and ceremonies to the young people. That, in turn, led back to the padres' opposition to such "devil-worship." How had it all started? It seemed to Gutierrez that it was much like the old riddle with no answer, about whether the chicken or the egg had come first.

Gutierrez would have preferred to stay entirely out of such conflict, but now his course of action had been chosen for him. He had been caught up and swept along on the winds of the conflict, with no real decision of his own. He was like the little wisps of dust that sometimes whirled across the sandy flats in the heat of summer. "Dust devils," some called them. A stray puff of breeze would pick up and whirl a puff of dust, making it dance unpredictably, zigzagging for some distance through the otherwise still sunlight of the afternoon. Yes, that was how he felt, he decided. He had no more control over his actions, over his life, in fact, than the crazily skittering puff of dust. He was being whirled helplessly toward . . . what?

He thought about María. She would in all probability be immune to most of the blame for his actions. They would question her, but she knew nothing to tell. If her husband did not return, she would undoubtedly join her sister's household after a while.

Mother of God, what was he thinking? Of course he would rejoin her. This conflict would be soon resolved, and he would be able to resume his life. He shook his head to clear it of the dark thoughts that had descended on him.

Late in the afternoon, Gutierrez' aching body had become so numb that it no longer seemed to matter. He had had no sleep at all, and from time to time almost dozed when the mare plodded along a level stretch. He was dozing in this manner when there was a shout and a series of excited calls between the others of the party. They halted, and the loose horses began to scatter into the brush to browse.

He focused his eyes to return to reality. Up ahead, on a low rise to the left of the trail, stood three natives. Apparently they had called out to halt the travelers, and now wished to talk. Turkey Foot was reining toward them. Out of curiosity and concern, Gutierrez kneed his horse forward to hear the conversation. Other natives were now appearing from behind brush and rocks.

"Buenos días," Turkey Foot was saying.

The tall man in the center responded in his own tongue, and Turkey Foot shrugged.

"I do not know your tongue," he said, again using Spanish.

He spoke a few words which Gutierrez did not understand, and the other shook his head irritably.

"Then it must be Spanish, *amigo,*" Turkey Foot concluded.

The man nodded reluctantly.

"We do not like to use Spanish," he explained. "Now, we saw you before. Where is the other one, your leader?"

"In Santa Fe. He was put in a cage, we are told."

"Where are the weapons he promised?"

Turkey Foot chose to ignore the question of such a promise.

"Our goods were taken by the soldiers. Our horses, too."

"But you . . ."

"We stole them back, and theirs too."

The other man laughed briefly, but then became serious.

"And you have no weapons but your own, only these and the horses?"

It was apparent that this was a great disappointment. The man's eyes roved over the scattered animals, and then he seemed to notice Gutierrez for the first time.

"Ah, you have a prisoner! Is this not the trader?"

"Yes, but he is not . . ."

"Good!" interrupted the other man. "We will kill him and send back his fat carcass to warn the others."

Terror gripped Gutierrez. If it had been possible he would have struck heels to his horse and fled, but he was unable to move. He should have gone back, he told himself. At least he would have been among his own. Now, to die here . . .

"No!" Turkey Foot spoke. His voice was quiet, but his tone was deadly. "This is our friend, who saved us from being in the cage, too. Now hear me!"

He raised his voice a little, to be well heard by the others.

"This Spaniard is one of us! Anyone who harms him answers to me!"

Turkey Foot rested a hand on the stone war club that dangled at his waist. Gutierrez recalled that Turkey Foot was of the slightly different tribe known as Head Splitters. Whether the natives on the hillside knew this or not, the significance of his gesture was not lost on them.

"Of course," the young chief agreed hastily. "Let it be as you say."

Gutierrez, who had broken into a cold sweat, now wiped his damp palms on his trousers. He felt a little better. In fact, now that the terror was over, he had a moment to think. Turkey Foot had defended him, treated him with respect. In spite of all his obvious shortcomings, he had been accepted, and Turkey Foot had made this quite plain to all.

It was a good feeling, the self-respect that came flowing over him. He straightened a little, and even his aching muscles seemed to respond to the new Gutierrez.

Turkey Foot was speaking again.

"Now," he asked firmly, "do you want these horses, or not?"

13

» » »

By earliest light, Red Feather was attempting to look at the loose window bar that formed part of their prison. He examined the construction of the opening, which was certainly well built and solid. A heavy wooden beam embedded in the adobe wall formed the sill of the opening, and holes had been bored to accept the lower ends of the iron bars. A similar beam across the top of the opening held the upper end of each bar.

He wiggled the loose bar experimentally. A few grains of dirt pattered on the sill again, from the upper end of the bar. In a short while, he had enough information to let him come to some conclusions.

The bar could be rotated in its sockets quite easily. Since each motion of any sort seemed to dislodge dirt at its upper end, the holes must reach completely through the wooden beam. At least this one did, at the top end. He lifted the bar straight up for the scant finger's width that was possible, and let it drop back. There was a hollow "thunk" of iron on wood. Ah, the hole at the bottom did *not* go completely through the sill. Then it must be only the upper end of the bar that did pass through. In that way, it could dislodge small amounts of crumbled dirt brick from above the window.

He worked at this theory a little longer. Yes, he found that the greatest amount of dirt fell to the sill when he pushed the bar upward and at the same time twisted it with a rotating motion. Soon he could see that he was making progress. The bar could be raised higher than before, by a tiny amount. He paused to evaluate the size of the opening. Yes, if this one bar was removed, there would be . . .

"What is it, Father?"

White Fox was impatient.

"If we can take this one bar out, there is room to climb through," Red Feather pointed.

"But it cannot be taken out!"

"Maybe so. See, it slides upward. When the lower end comes up, out of the wood, maybe we can bend the bar enough to slide it back down and out."

"*Aiee!* But can it move up that far?"

Fox pointed to the beam at the sill. It was more than a hand's span thick. The lower end of the bar might rest in a hole as deep as only two fingers' width, or it might go nearly all the way through the beam. In that case, it would take days of patient twisting to displace that much adobe.

"I do not know," Red Feather answered, "but we have to try. We can both work at it. Not now. We will work only after dark."

The other prisoner, who had still not established any communication, now became interested. He rose and walked to the window to test the bar. He turned with a broad smile, nodding eagerly. He pointed to himself and then to the bar, making a twisting motion.

There were none of the signs of the plains' hand-sign talk, but his meaning was clear. He would help.

Red Feather nodded, and then made the sign for sleep. The other man looked puzzled. Red Feather pointed to the floor and closed his eyes.

"Wait until night."

Maybe the man understood a little Spanish, he thought. Their companion smiled and nodded agreement, but they were still not certain about the Spanish. They brushed the loose dirt from the sill and sat down to await the dull routine of the day.

That night the three took turns working on the bar. The combination of lifting and twisting was an odd and unusual use of the muscles. It could not be done for very long at a time before the arms became stiff and cramped and it was necessary to change position. After a few turns at the window, Red Feather began to think that he could not even raise his aching arms above shoulder height again.

By dawn after the first night of work, it was apparent that they had made only a little progress. The bar could be raised a little higher, but only another finger's breadth. Discouraged, Red Feather looked at the heavy sill. There was no way to tell how deeply the bar was imbedded. They might have only another finger to go, or even less. Or, it could be that they were only starting.

One thing bothered him considerably. The progress seemed to have slowed. The bar was not dislodging as much dirt as it had at first. He thought about that at great length during that day, and finally decided a possible reason. He had once observed the construction of a lodge at Blue Corn's pueblo. They had prepared a large quantity of mud, stirring it with their feet, and mixing in dried grasses. This substance was then shaped into square blocks and allowed to harden in the sun. Later, they were stacked to form the walls of the lodge, with wet mud between the blocks to stick them together.

So, he reasoned, at first the bar had been loosening some of the stick-together mud. It would be softer than the sun-baked blocks with dried grasses. They had now reached a baked block that lay over the upper beam, and the going was slower.

This discovery produced mixed feelings. It would be slower, but at least there was a reason. But he wondered with a feeling of dread whether there might be any small stones in the mud of the blocks. A pebble the size of his thumb could effectively stop progress completely, if their bar encountered such an obstacle.

Ah, well, they could only continue to try. They had no other alternative.

When he was not thinking about the window, Red Feather worried about the others. There had been no word from Gutierrez, which seemed odd. He had thought that the trader would find some way to contact them, to let them know if Turkey Foot and the rest of the party had escaped. He had lost track of how many sleeps they had been caged. Surely, if there had been a skirmish, the jailers would have taken opportunity to gloat.

With this idea in mind, he tried to talk to the jailer who brought their food.

"*Buenos días, señor*. Do you know what happened to the others of our party?"

The soldier grunted, then chuckled.

"You had best worry about yourselves!"

Ah, this is good, thought Red Feather. If they had

been captured or killed, this man would know, and could not have resisted bragging about it. So they must have escaped. Even now, they were probably at Blue Corn's, waiting for him and White Fox to come.

This, in turn, made him think of Moonflower. He thought of her often, and how difficult this must be for her. He had no doubt that she knew of their capture. The communication of the pueblo people had always been a wonder to him. Information, it seemed, traveled through the mountains like the flight of an eagle. Yes, she would know of events in Santa Fe, even before Turkey Foot and the others reached the pueblo.

Still, he wished he could talk to Gutierrez, to know how things stood. It was not knowing that was frustrating. Maybe, he thought frequently, it would be better if the party from the plains would go ahead and start home. They were in relative safety at the pueblo, but they had their families to think of. Moonflower could stay with her parents, or return to the plains and her other children. He shook his head in frustration.

Ah, well, he finally decided, they could make their plans without him. They must. He would think of other things, of this present problem, of how to bend the window bar. And of their strange, silent fellow prisoner.

The man was cooperative, worked well, was not unpleasant to be with. Red Feather wished that he had asked the old man more about him during their short time together. Maybe he had not known, either. He wondered some about the old man, where he was and what had happened to him. He must have been released.

Then, as he rested his aching arms one night, an alarming thought came to him. Suppose this silent man who shared their cell was an ally of the Spanish. Had he been planted there to try to listen to their talk, to spy on them?

Red Feather watched the man's dim shape at the window, and listened to the soft scrape of iron on the hard-baked adobe. He must speak to White Fox about this. They would have to be careful.

Then he almost chuckled aloud. What did they have to be careful about? They had told the soldiers the truth, and there was nothing more that could be said, nothing different. Their only real crime was the escape attempt, and the silent one already knew about that. If he was a spy, Red Feather thought, he would probably let them almost finish, and then tell the guards.

Well, there was nothing that could be done now. They would continue to work, and take each day as it came. After all, what else could one do?

The silent one stopped in his labor, and sank to the floor. Red Feather stepped to take his place. His shoulders ached so that he could hardly raise his arms above his head to grasp the bar. Wearily, he began to rotate it.

14
» » »

It was apparent to Gutierrez that the two groups with whom he rode were quite different. He had realized this before, that the traders and the people of the pueblos were of separate tribes, but their vastly different customs had never come to his attention. He simply had not thought much about it.

Now, that situation was driven home to him quite forcefully. These two groups of natives were so different that they could not even talk to each other. They were as different as French and Spanish. No, even more so. Most French and Spanish could speak a little of each other's tongue. Well, in the border country, anyway. But these two groups were forced to converse in Spanish, which was the tongue of neither. That, in turn, was resented by the pueblo people, who made no secret of the fact that they hated all things Spanish, even the language. He was certain that he would have been killed just for *being* Spanish if Turkey Foot had not intervened. It was a strange and frightening feeling.

On the other hand, it was fortunate for Gutierrez that they were forced to use Spanish. He could understand all that was said between the two groups. Unfortunately, he knew little of either of the native tongues, so discussion within either group was a mystery. It was especially disconcerting to watch and listen while the men from the pueblos argued among themselves, occasionally casting dark glances his way. What were they talking about?

He also suspected that the two groups did not fully trust each other. They stayed apart, drawing aside with others of their own kind when they stopped to rest or to camp for the night. Gutierrez was frightened. He dreaded constantly what would happen without the presence of the men from the plains. He was certain that the others would turn on him in an instant. Consequently, he stayed as close as possible to Turkey Foot at all times. He knew that he was annoying to Turkey Foot, but he would rather face that annoyance than the vengeance of the men from the pueblos.

That, too, worried him. Why? he asked himself. Why did they cast dark glances at him, suggestive of the fate he would meet if they had their way? He had always treated them fairly, but it did not seem to matter to these men. Of course, he realized that it was partly because they were strangers to him. He did not see a man with whom he had ever had dealings. They must have come from outside the immediate area. Since he did not know them, they naturally did not know him, either. It was hurtful to his pride, though, to be automatically considered an enemy. He would have hoped that his reputation for fairness was well known, but that, too, did not seem to matter. The only thing that did matter was the fact that he was a Spaniard. And, he resented their attitude about that. He had a certain amount of pride in his own heritage.

Who did these upstart savages think they were, anyway?

It had been decided that part of the pueblo party would assume control of the horse herd, except for those being ridden. They would take the animals somewhere else, but were quite vague about where. They were quite vague about everything, when it came down to it. It appeared that they wanted to give no more information than necessary, either to him or to Turkey Foot's party.

He also had the impression that possession of the horses was more symbolic than useful. A number of the mountain people scorned the use of the horse. It was some time before he realized that for the purists among the rebels, even the horse was a symbol of the hated Spanish.

There had been no clear-cut decision as to what Turkey Foot and his party would do after their arrival at Blue Corn's. Originally, they had planned to wait there for Red Feather, assuming he would soon be released. Now, there was no way to know. Gutierrez had an uneasy feeling, too late, that their raid on the horse herd might have affected the prisoners' chances. He was unhappy that he had been unable to get word to Red Feather. At the time when he should have been doing so, he was in the midst of the raid and the ensuing escape, carried along by events over which he had no control.

That feeling of lack of control was growing rapidly. He was riding with these natives, with no clear idea of where they were going, or why. What would happen when they reached the pueblo? He would have to help explain to Red Feather's wife . . . Mother of God, how and why had he become involved in this? More to the point, *why?* What would happen next?

A frightening thought struck him. What if, after their arrival at the pueblo, Turkey Foot and the others decided to return to their own country without waiting for Red Feather? Or, what if he was never released? Even if Red Feather did rejoin them, they would immediately leave for the plains, and where would he, Gutierrez, be? Any way he looked at it, there was a good chance that he might be stranded at the outlying pueblo with no protection and no clear idea of where he was.

It had started as a great adventure and a chance for a bit of retribution against the soldiers who had confiscated and padlocked his store. From there, his world had seemed to fall apart under him. He now saw no way out. Sooner or later, he would have to return to Santa Fe, and there would be questions and accusations. But now, he was already thinking that that might be preferable to being stranded among strangers, some of whom would quite plainly like to kill him.

To add to his uneasiness, his physical discomfort was a major part of his day. Still sore and aching in every joint, he had developed other sources of misery. He had always been a man to sweat profusely. One good thing about this land was that sweat dried rapidly, producing a cooling effect. Only now, it did not work. Rivers of sweat poured from his skin, puddled in every wrinkle and crevice of his plump body. There it blended with blown dust and sand, becoming an abrasive mixture. His underarms, his groin, every fold of belly fat around his midriff was chafed and galled. In addition, the inside of each plump thigh was rubbed raw from crotch to knee from the motion of the horse. The salt sweat made the abraded area sting like fire.

The sun on his back was a torment, too. Especially, one area over his right flank seemed sensitive to the unrelenting rays. Gradually, he became aware of a mild stinging sensation, and reached back to scratch the offending place. To his surprise, his searching fingers encountered bare skin. There was a long rip in his cotton shirt, from shoulder to waist.

It did not really concern him, the sun would not actually be harmful. That stripe would soon burn as brown as his face and hands. It did bother him, however, to be wearing a shirt that was almost totally destroyed. It did not seem decent. María would not approve. He smiled to himself, to realize that such a thing would concern him, with all the other problems that confronted his immediate future.

At the next stop, he took off the shirt to examine it. Yes, there was the rip. He did not know how it had happened, or when. During one of his heroic efforts to wriggle his bulk to the back of the horse, most likely.

Turkey Foot walked past and chuckled.

"That shirt is dead, *amigo*. I had an extra, but it is gone, with all else. We will get you one at the pueblo."

"Thank you," Gutierrez smiled.

It appeared that someone *was* concerned about his welfare, after all. Yes, Turkey Foot would help him. He felt better as he painfully remounted. In spirit, at least.

15

» » »

"**I** would wish to think so, but my heart tells me no," Blue Corn said sadly. "No, the Hairfaces will not let them go."

Gutierrez nodded.

"This is true, I think. They will hold them because of the weapons."

Moonflower was crying quietly.

"Is there any way to release them?" she asked Turkey Foot.

He shrugged.

"Who knows? I do not understand any of this," he said in disgust. "Maybe they will know."

He jerked a thumb at the area along the stream where the war party of rebels was camped.

"Let us ask," agreed Blue Corn.

He called to a youth who was loitering to see the strangers.

"Blackbird, come here!"

The young man trotted over, pleased to be noticed by one of the Elders.

"Go and ask Spotted Owl, the leader of those men, to join us here," he requested.

Blackbird loped off, eager to be involved.

"Ah, I fear more trouble," Blue Corn said sadly. "My visions are not good."

"Not good, Father?" Moonflower asked anxiously. "How?"

"Much trouble, between our people and the Hairfaces. I see more, more bloodshed; it is a bad thing."

Spotted Owl was walking across the open space toward them.

"Maybe he will know something of that, too," mused Blue Corn.

The conversation was in Spanish, so that Turkey Foot and Gutierrez could participate. Spotted Owl showed his resentment, but nodded grudgingly. Turkey Foot stated the problem, how to free Red Feather and his son, or at least to find out about them.

They would have expected almost any reaction except the one they got. They were surprised to see Spotted Owl bristle with alarm and, yes, *anger.*

"No!" he snapped. "It cannot be!"

"But we must try!" Turkey Foot now bristled, too.

"No, you must not!" Spotted Owl insisted again.

"But why?"

The other man became sullen.

"I cannot tell."

Blue Corn was astonished. What was going on, here? He did not know this Spotted Owl well, but got a strong feeling that there was much here that did not meet the eye. Something, perhaps, that he did not wish Turkey Foot to know? Or Gutierrez? Ah, yes, that must be it! They did not trust the Spaniard. Blue Corn spoke in his own tongue.

"What is it, Owl?

The other man paused before he answered, and even then spoke with great hesitation.

"I cannot tell, even you."

Blue Corn very nearly became angered, this conversation was so frustrating. With effort, he regained his composure. He must walk softly, now.

"My brother," he said soothingly, "what is it that you cannot tell even an Elder of our own people?"

Spotted Owl looked him straight in the eyes, and at last drew a deep breath.

"Forgive me, Wise One. I am not concerned that you know, but these others . . . they must not be in Santa Fe when . . ." He paused again. "They will spoil the plan. And this fat Spaniard . . . he must not be allowed to know anything at all. Some already want to kill him."

Blue Corn stared in wonder.

"What are you talking about? Know *what?*"

"About the plan. Popé is about to drive the Spanish out."

"Out of the town?" the astonished Blue Corn asked.

"More! Out of our land, back to where they came from!"

"But . . . when?"

"Soon. We will wait here for the signal. Any day, now."

"How is it that I have not heard of this, Owl?"

"It has not been known to many. I am to tell you when the time comes, and ask for the help of your young men."

Ah, yes, thought Blue Corn, it must come to this. He had long tried to deny this reality, but now he must face it. Yes, he could understand how they felt they must silence Gutierrez for their own safety. He glanced over at the trader. What a pitiful thing. Even with a night's rest and a new shirt of pueblo pattern, the man looked stiff and sore, tired, and harmless. Yes, harmless. Blue Corn could not condone the idea of killing this man so that he would present no danger.

"This Spaniard is no danger to you," he found himself saying. "Look at him . . . helpless."

"But he is one of *them*," Spotted Owl hissed. "We must drive out all things Spanish."

"Drive out, yes. But kill him? It is not needed. And what of these others?"

Spotted Owl seemed at a loss for a moment, mildly confused.

"I do not know," he admitted, "but I do not trust them, either. They trade with the Hairfaces."

"Yet they gave you horses!"

"Yes, that is true. But . . ."

"Owl, it is two of their own people whom they wish to free. These are also my daughter's husband and son."

"But they will spoil the plan!"

He paused, and an idea seemed to come to him.

"Would they fight with us when the time comes?" he asked. "To free their people?"

"I do not know, Owl. Let us ask them."

"No! They must know nothing!"

"How can we know what they will do without asking them?" Blue Corn asked calmly.

"Yes," agreed Spotted Owl reluctantly, "you are right. But only their leader, the one called Turkey. And not the Spaniard."

"He can do no harm," Blue Corn insisted. "If he becomes a threat, we can kill him at any time." He was trying to buy time for Gutierrez. "Come, let us talk to Turkey Foot," he suggested.

There was some trouble convincing Gutierrez to leave Turkey Foot's side so that they could talk. Finally the trader agreed to stay in the lodge while the other three walked outside. Moonflower smiled at Gutierrez reassuringly and pointed to a seat by the fireplace.

Outside, Blue Corn spoke to Turkey Foot, "*Amigo*, we must talk. Tell him, Owl."

Spotted Owl rapidly outlined the upcoming plans for purging the Spanish, while Turkey Foot's eyes became wide and round.

"*Aiee!*" he said softly. "I see, now. But we must get Red Feather out of there. When does this happen?"

"We do not know. Someone will come to tell us, and then we move on to Santa Fe."

Turkey Foot turned to Blue Corn.

"Your young men go, too?"

"I do not know. Some of them, maybe."

"But you will not, yourself?"

Blue Corn answered slowly.

"I think not. I am old, but even so, killing is not the way. If this fails, and the Hairfaces come . . ."

He did not need to finish. There were pueblos where the Hairfaces had killed indiscriminantly, maimed the survivors, and sent the women and children into slavery.

"That is *why* we must fight!" urged Spotted Owl.

Blue Corn nodded reluctantly.

"Maybe so. Fight, or leave," he murmured, almost to himself.

"But first, we get Red Feather free," Turkey Foot

insisted. "Look, we will join you in this fight, if you will help us free him when we get there."

"Of course," agreed Spotted Owl. "We can use fighting men. Do you know where he is caged?"

"No, but Gutierrez does."

"No!" snapped Spotted Owl firmly. "He must not be there!"

"But only he knows. Listen, he showed us how to steal the horses. He can help us."

Spotted Owl paused, then spoke.

"I do not trust him."

"We do not have to trust him," Turkey Foot insisted. "He will be where we can watch him. If his heart is bad, any one of us can kill him."

"But he would have to know the plan," argued Spotted Owl.

"Not all of it," observed Blue Corn. "He could know only that we were trying to free the prisoners. I will go with you, not to fight, but to watch the Spaniard."

Turkey Foot and Owl looked questioningly at each other, unable to find fault with this suggestion.

"It is good!" stated Turkey Foot, almost triumphantly.

Spotted Owl smiled. He had done little smiling until now.

"Yes," he agreed. "But we tell no one, for now. Only we three. Agreed?"

The others nodded.

Blue Corn was not entirely pleased with the compromise. He felt that all of them were being drawn into the center of this whirlpool of events beyond their control. He would have preferred not to be included, but he felt that he must. Gutierrez had risked his life to try to help Red Feather and White Fox. If for no other reason, he, Blue Corn, must go with the others to make sure that no one harmed the trader.

If, of course, he could prevent it. That in itself seemed highly questionable. He must seek more visions, pray more prayers. Why must trouble come searching for those who did not seek it? The whole thing was like ashes in his mouth.

He would do almost anything to help the family of his daughter, but after that . . . somehow his thoughts of the future were not clear. He could not see his role in the reestablishment of the Old Ways.

Or, as far as that went, in the attack on the Hairfaces to banish them forever from the town of Santa Fe.

16

» » »

When the word finally arrived, the coming purge was already known to all. It was not discussed openly, of course. It was a secretive thing, the men of the pueblo in casual contact with those of the rebel band. It could not be many days of such living before conversations turned to the purpose of the rebels' presence. They, in addition, wished to recruit fighting men.

The last to realize the full import of the situation were Turkey Foot's plainsmen. The language barrier prevented open discussion, and in addition they were not yet quite trusted. Still, Turkey Foot had felt it unfair not to inform his companions, and had let drop a hint here and there. That was all that was necessary. The entire pueblo and both groups camped nearby were well aware before long that events of major importance were expected.

Gutierrez was the one person who really had no one to talk to about pending events. He could feel the tenseness, and sensed that there was an undercurrent of secrecy here. He wanted very badly to be accepted and respected. There had been a certain change, after the conversation from which he was excluded. Somehow he felt a lessening of the danger to him. He was tolerated more easily, even by the rebel camp. They were not exactly friendly, but at least there were not the murderous side glances that had frightened him so much.

Everyone seemed to be doing nothing in particular, merely waiting. Waiting for what? Somehow he felt that it was a specific event, but he was unsure. What was it, and how would it relate to him? He was still undecided as to what he would like to do, if he were able to choose. He must return to Santa Fe eventually, he knew. It was necessary to inquire as to the store, and his own legal status. He did not believe that his part in the horse raid was known, and he still hoped to use the kidnap story. Yes, that should extricate him, if he played it right.

He had still not figured out what everyone was waiting for. His own future was so uncertain that there was an urgency to know what to expect, but all attempts at inquiry were met with rebuff or with silence.

"When the time comes," Turkey Foot told him nonchalantly.

So Gutierrez waited. When the word finally came, activity began to increase and excitement spread. The bewildered trader sought out Turkey Foot.

"What is it, *amigo*, what is happening?"

Turkey Foot led him aside.

"We are going to attack the Hairfaces at Santa Fe."

Gutierrez paled and became short of breath. He wished now that he did not know. Then anger rose in him. His was a bigger risk than that of anyone here.

"Why was I not told?" he demanded.

"They did not trust you."

"*Trust* me? What did they want me to do? Those are my people!"

Turkey Foot nodded.

"Yes, *amigo,* and that is the problem. You might want to warn them. But if you did not know . . ."

Gutierrez could partially understand. Yes, he might be expected to try to warn the town, but could not if he knew nothing. So to prevent such a problem, Turkey Foot had told him nothing.

An alarming thought struck him. Why had he been told now? This implied that he was no longer a threat. Did they intend to kill him? His palms began to sweat and his voice was pinched and falsetto when he spoke.

"Then why do you tell me now?"

"We need you," said Turkey Foot simply.

"*Need* me? I cannot fight my own people!"

"No, no, not to fight. You must take us to where Red Feather is held. We will free him when the others strike."

"And what then?"

He still saw much potential danger. There might be other bands of rebels, who would not know him, and who would be killing Spaniards. He began to tremble.

"I cannot do this thing, señor."

"You can," Turkey Foot said firmly. "You will." Then he softened a little. "For our friend Red Feather? Then you go where you wish."

Yes, thought Gutierrez. To the protection of the soldiers. Yes, this could turn out well. He would feel better back in the familiar surroundings of the town. He could go home, after the hostilities were over, home to María. He felt better.

"Yes, I can show you. You will tell the others that I will do no harm to anyone?"

"Yes, *amigo.* I will tell them. You are to be protected. Stay close to me. Now, get your horse. We will be leaving soon."

Gutierrez felt better again. He felt safe with Turkey Foot, and now that he knew what was happening, his confidence returned. It was reassuring to think that he could be of some use in the rescue of their mutual friend, Red Feather. Best of all, no one had asked him, or even expected him, to take sides in the coming conflict. His own people might do so, of course.

Odd, he thought. Of the several different tribes or nations involved in the confrontation, only one would possibly insist that he see things as they did. That one was his own. And to an extent he did see the problems of the Spanish colonials. After all, he *was* one of them. Supplies were not arriving regularly, and this made everyone irritable. It was not a good time for the padres to try to force the Church on the Elders in the pueblos.

For that matter, it was difficult for him to see how a person could be forced to think in any particular way. It seemed to him that someone could be forced to do certain things, to act in certain ways. He could even be told how he must eat and drink and dress. But how could he be forced to *believe* anything other than what he believed? It was too easy to say yes, I agree, but inside, to say to one's self, no, that is wrong.

The people of the pueblos, it had always seemed to him, were quite willing to let anyone think what he liked. Their attitude plainly said, "What you think is not mine to be concerned over, it is yours." He had not quite gotten to the point where he saw the other side of that same attitude: "Since I do not interfere with your thoughts and beliefs, you have no right to interfere with mine." He was only aware that Popé, the troublemaker, was resisting the attempts of the padres to stop the ceremonies in the kivas. It was unfortunate that they could not come to a meeting of the minds on this. True, it would be difficult to persuade the priests, particularly that new one who seemed to have been responsible for Red Feather's imprisonment. Equally inflexible was Popé, still resentful, probably, over his own imprisonment last year. There seemed no easy solution.

Gutierrez scratched his belly through his new shirt as he walked out to fetch his horse. The tightly woven tunic was quite comfortable, loose-fitting and airy. He had belted it on the outside of his trousers, after the custom of the pueblo people, and was enjoying the feel of the garment. His skin had healed, even the badly chafed areas along his inner thighs. The chafed spots were peeling now, however, and itched from time to time. In retrospect, the journey on the horse had not been so bad. It had been mostly the unaccustomed use of all his parts that had caused his misery. He would do better on the return trip, he was sure.

His horse, after a few halfhearted attempts to escape, allowed itself to be caught. Gutierrez knotted the rawhide thong around the animal's lower jaw as Turkey Foot had taught him, led the horse over to a rock, and swung a leg over. The horse exhaled audibly, but resignedly moved toward the lodges. Gutierrez would place a saddle pad on the creature there. He felt much more confident about riding now. He felt more confident about everything now, actually.

He wondered if there might be some way in which he could help to smooth out the conflict between these groups of people, his own and the natives. They should be able to cooperate. They needed each other.

17

» » »

From time to time Red Feather had attempted to initiate conversation with the jailers when they brought food, or when they carried out the bucket which the prisoners were allowed to use for bodily functions.

Sometimes in the summer heat the odor in the cell became quite oppressive, as the jailers neglected that unpleasant task. Occasionally, it seemed that the bucket must overflow. Once, when the guards made no move to empty it, the silent man with whom they shared the cell picked up the bucket and tossed its contents out the window. This produced unpleasant results all around. The guards rushed in, administered a beating, and shouted threats. They seemed to have no doubt as to the identity of the culprit. Red Feather had the impression that such an incident had happened before.

Another bad result, however, was that the work at the window bar became more unpleasant. They attempted to clean off the sill with wisps of the straw bedding, which they then tossed out the window. This was only partly successful. At least, the guards seemed more dedicated to the task of removing the bucket more regularly. They may have been severely reprimanded for such an incident.

The silent man remained silent, except for occasional grunts, and that continued to be the entire content of their conversation. "The One-Who-Never-Speaks," White Fox had begun to call him, in their own tongue. This was soon shortened to Never-Speaks. Red Feather was still mildly suspicious that he might be a spy. The incident of the thrown bucket of dung and urine, and the resulting beating, had seemed to discourage the theory. Still, would that not be an excellent way to throw the other prisoners off guard? Red Feather was still reserving his opinion.

He continued to speak to the guards at every opportunity, hoping to glean information. Sometimes he could catch a scrap of conversation from the hallway, but the guards were mostly concerned with their own problems, such as rations and pay. Once they exchanged news of a patrol that had been attacked and casualties inflicted, but there was no further discussion. It was apparent, however, that a change was in the air, that the treatment the prisoners received was more abusive, the few words that were exchanged more gruff and threatening. This obvious change led Red Feather to hope that there would be no open hostilities. That would present a great threat to the welfare of the prisoners.

One guard seemed a trifle less abusive than the others, and Red Feather decided to concentrate on trying to talk to that one. The man was far from friendly, but there were little lines around his eyes and at the corners of his mouth that seemed to indicate a basic good humor. After a few days of brief greeting, the man actually answered Red Feather's *"buenos días."* After that, he frequently did so, though sometimes with only a grunt.

Red Feather was elated at even this small show of response, and continued to cultivate the sparse conversation. Finally one morning he felt secure enough to ask the question that had bothered him since their imprisonment.

"Señor, why does this man never speak?"

The jailer glanced at Never-Speaks and back to Red Feather, his expression dark and foreboding.

"Because he is wiser than you. And because he has no tongue. He lost it by using it too much. It would be best to remember that."

It was the longest speech that any jailer had ever given, and certainly the most significant. Red Feather recoiled in shock. The other prisoner had had his tongue cut out, for using it too much.

This put an immediate end to the attempts at communication, but spurred renewed activity at the barred window. Finally there came the night when White Fox roused his father excitedly.

"The iron bar! It is free!" he whispered.

Red Feather jumped up to feel the lower end of the bar in the predawn darkness. Yes, it was true. The bar could now be raised high enough in the upper socket to clear the sill at the bottom. Now, if only they could bend it. He grasped the bar near the sill and pulled it toward him. The metal yielded only a little.

"We will wait," Red Feather whispered. "It is too near light."

He pointed to the yellow glow along the eastern horizon.

"Tonight," he told his son.

Never-Speaks, who had risen now to see what was happening, felt the bar and nodded happily.

This seemed like the longest day since their imprisonment. The waiting for night to come so that their escape could be carried out was an eternity. They talked a little, in their own tongue.

"If we are separated," Red Feather advised, "we will meet at your grandfather's pueblo. Can you find it?"

"Of course," White Fox answered.

The boy seemed a little indignant that such a matter should even be questioned.

"What about Never-Speaks?" he asked.

"I do not know. He will do as he chooses."

They waited that night until the usual activity in the hallway quieted. After what seemed a very long time, the guards changed shifts. There were the customary sounds of the incoming jailer shuffling around, preparing for his lonely vigil. Finally, he seemed to settle in, and before long they could hear the rhythmic snoring that said it was time to act.

The thought went through Red Feather's mind that maybe they would be unable to bend the bar. Then all their nights of work would be for nothing. No, they *must* find a way to do it. The snores from the corridor were regular and deep now. Red Feather rose and approached the window. Carefully, he raised the bar to its highest point and wiggled it to make certain that the lower end was free.

It was a clumsy angle, reaching higher than his head to seize and try to pull. The bar would give only a little. He began to feel panic. Suppose they bent the bar, but not enough to draw it out. They could not replace it. Then it would be noticed, and . . . he did not know what might happen next, but it would not be good. He paused, panting after the exertion. Never-Speaks stepped over to try, then White Fox, but when Red Feather again took his turn, there was very little change in the shape and position of the bar. There was a slight bend, the width of a finger, preventing the lower end from dropping back into the socket. They now must continue, and there was no turning back. He gave a mighty heave, with no apparent result.

He paused to think a moment. The problem was that they could not exert full strength in an awkward pull overhead. If they only had a rope, or . . . No sooner had he thought of that solution than he was untying and removing his leggings. The soft-tanned buckskin would be strong yet pliable. Quickly, he twisted the leather into a short, stout rope and looped it around the bar. He gave an experimental pull. Yes, he could plainly feel the give of the iron bar.

Still, it was not quite enough. He tried again. The bar would give but then spring back. There must be a stronger, more prolonged pull than he could deliver alone.

"Help me!" he whispered to White Fox.

The young man joined him, and the two gave a long pull, straining every muscle to its limit. He could feel some motion at the window, but could not be certain. Was it the bending of the bar, or merely the stretch of the improvised rope?

"Stop!" he whispered finally.

The rope went slack, and he reached to feel the bar. Yes! It had moved, nearly a hand's span. Never-Speaks reached up too, excited by the progress.

This time, he, too, tried to assist with the pull. It became apparent very quickly that there was motion as they began to strain. Only a little more, now. Suddenly the buckskin rope went slack. Off balance, the three men tumbled backward in an awkward pile as the smooth leather slid from the lower end of the bar and fell to the floor with them. Almost at the same time the iron bar, released from sideways pressure, slid downward, out of the upper socket, and dropped to the floor. There was a thud when it struck the hard-packed earth, and a metallic, ringing vibration.

The snores in the corridor had stopped, and the sentry was stirring. Red Feather scrambled to his feet, pushing White Fox toward the window. He boosted the young man up, head first through the opening, and heard him strike the ground outside.

He turned to look for Never-Speaks. By the light of the lantern now bobbing in the corridor, he saw their companion stooping to pick up the iron bar.

"What is going on in there?" called the jailer.

There were sounds of his approach, and more sounds of running footsteps in the corridor. A face appeared at the little window in the door, but it was apparent that the jailer could not see well enough. He muttered a curse, and the rattle of keys was followed by the metallic click of the lock.

Never-Speaks was pointing to the window, grunting unintelligibly as he pushed Red Feather toward it. Almost before he had time to think, he found himself boosted up to the opening. He wriggled through and dropped, springing back up to assist their companion. The door was swinging wide, flooding the cell with yellow lantern light. He reached a hand to help Never-Speaks.

But the other man was not at the window. Red Feather watched as he took one long step toward the door, swinging the bent iron bar with all his strength.

The improvised weapon struck the guard across the face. There was a sharp crack of breaking bone, and the man went down heavily. His limbs twitched for a moment as his reluctant spirit struggled to remain in the dying body.

Now Never-Speaks sprang back toward the window. He grasped Red Feather's extended hand and pulled himself up. Red Feather could see the reflection on the roof poles of lanterns in the hall, and could hear shouts and running steps. Never-Speaks now had his head and shoulders in the window, and was wriggling through.

"Come on, hurry," Red Feather urged, still attempting to help pull the man through the opening.

There was a deafening roar, and the hand that grasped his gave a convulsive spasm and went limp. The lifeless body of Never-Speaks slid back through the window and dropped inside, while Red Feather, off balance, fell flat. It was a moment before Red Feather, ears ringing from the concussion, realized what had happened. The thunder-stick! *Aiee*, what chance did they have? With their powerful medicine, the weapons could kill at a distance.

"Run!" he yelled to White Fox.

"Is he . . . ?"

"We cannot help him. Come!"

He jumped to his feet and sprinted away, White Fox at his side. Quickly, he glanced at the sky, orienting himself by the Seven Hunters and the Real-star. He drew in a great lungful of fresh night air, the air of freedom.

18

» » »

The night air of the mountains carried a chill, even in summer. Red Feather estimated that at home on the plains, this must be the Red Moon, hottest and driest of the year. He had lost track of time during their imprisonment, where one day blended into another with few differences. Mostly those were distinguished by some being more unpleasant than usual. But enough days had passed that it must be the Red Moon.

Even so, nights were always cold in the mountains. They had noticed it before. At home in the grasslands, there was a cooling of the world at night, a comforting relief from the Red Moon's blazing heat. Frequently, especially in the more western areas of the Sacred Hills, it was necessary to seek a robe sometimes until Sun Boy's torch began to warm the day again.

Here in the mountains, the chill of night was more than that. It was crisp, knifelike, and quite uncomfortable. Red Feather's teeth chattered, both from cold and excitement, as they ran through the deserted streets toward the edge of the town. Behind them, there was a growing noise and commotion as the soldiers roused to organize pursuit. There were shouts and curses. A musket boomed, the blast closely followed by the squeal of an injured pig. Some soldier had fired at a moving shadow in the darkness.

They ran on, the sounds becoming fainter behind them as distance widened. Once clear of the last lodges, they stopped for a moment to catch a breath. Red Feather found that he was weak, his legs threatening to give way. They must keep moving, before their muscles began to stiffen and cramp from the unaccustomed activity. He had not foreseen this, the weakness that would come from lack of exercise and poor food in the dingy cell of the Hairfaces. He was breathing hard, and the recovery was much slower than he had expected. His teeth started to chatter again from the cold.

"Here, Father, put on your leggings," White Fox was saying.

"You have them?"

"Yes. I tossed them out the window before we came out."

Red Feather had not noticed, in the excitement. He took the twisted wad of buckskin and shook the leggings free. The shape was distorted from inappropriate use, but it would conform again with wear. Gratefully, he pulled the garment on, and tied the thongs at the waist. He began to feel better, his aching legs protected now against the chill of the night breeze.

Now they must move on. There was no sign of immediate pursuit, and probably would not be until daylight. By then, they would cover all the distance possible. He wondered for a moment if the Hairfaces had any skilled trackers. He tried to remember the patrols of the Spanish. He had always been so impressed by the showy uniforms and rigid discipline of the troops, he had not noticed. They had surely had wolves out, but he could not remember. Were they uniformed soldiers? Or did the soldiers use guides and trackers as wolves?

Red Feather was a little disgusted with himself. He should have noted these things on his many visits here. Turkey Foot would have. So would Woodchuck, or Sky-Eyes. It was a serious oversight, but an understandable one, he felt. These Hairfaces, with whom they had long traded, were to be considered allies, like the Head Splitters. There had been no reason, until now, to evaluate them as potential enemies. Now, that had suddenly changed, from one visit to the next. Red Feather and his party had been treated with dishonor. Their property had been stolen, and he and White Fox had been imprisoned.

He wondered what had happened to the others. None had been captured, he thought, or they would surely have heard, through the guards. But what about Gutierrez? The trader should have returned with news, but had never come. Something must have interfered. For a moment, Red Feather considered going back for a look at the trader's store. But, no, it was too dangerous.

They would make their way to Blue Corn's, and he could tell them the answers to their questions. Maybe, even, the rest of their party would still be there. No, probably not, he decided. They would have gone home by now.

"Come, we must be far away by dawn," he told White Fox.

He pointed to the dark bulk of the mountains to the north.

"That is broken country. Rocky, with many places to hide. We will go that way."

"Would not the trail be faster?"

"Yes, but if they follow us on horses, they can travel faster than we would. No, we will stay in the rocks. It will be safer. We have no weapons, even."

White Fox nodded. They moved on, finding their way by the dim starlight, and heading toward the Real-star. By the time the yellow-gray of dawn began to lend its ghostly light, the scatter of adobe structures that made up the town of Santa Fe was far behind.

They stopped to rest after Sun Boy was nearly overhead. There had been no sign of pursuit. The excitement of the escape had subsided, and both were exhausted from lack of sleep and from the unusual effort.

"You sleep now," Red Feather suggested. "I will watch."

"When will you sleep?"

"After you wake. You can watch then. It is better if we travel mostly at night."

White Fox nodded. He curled up in the sand, his back against a red boulder, and was quickly asleep.

Red Feather selected a spot to sit and watch. He had chosen the place for their rest stop with care, protected from the rear by a sheer cliff of stone. Below them stretched a jumble of boulders, sloping toward the foothills and the open plain beyond. He could sit here and see any motion within a half day's journey. The town itself was not visible, hidden behind the folds of the foothills.

It was good, he thought, that there was no pursuit. It would have been easy to evade the soldiers, but he was glad that it was unnecessary. He wondered at some length about it. He had been right about the tension in the air, he told himself. The smoldering coals of trouble, fanned by an incident or two, would break into flame. The rapid response of the jailers to the escape, their readiness to shoot the prisoners, told the same story. He wondered if the escape might be one of the incidents that would ignite more trouble. But what else could they have done?

He wondered, too, about poor Never-Speaks. What had been the nature of the man's offense? There were many things about all this that he did not understand. What had happened to the old man who had shared their cell at first? He wanted to think that the Hairfaces had released him, but their treatment of Never-Speaks . . . *aiee*, they might easily have killed him!

Red Feather watched an antelope tiptoe down to water at the spring below the slope, a bow shot away. She must have suspected their presence, because she kept lifting her head nervously to stare and sniff the air. Her fawn followed closely, never straying far away. It was good to see that the world had not changed while they had been separated from it. He considered trying to kill one or the other of the animals for meat. They had no food of any kind. He quickly abandoned the idea. They had no weapons, either.

No, they would have to make their way to the safety of Blue Corn's pueblo, probably with empty stomachs. They had drunk deeply at the spring, and it had been good. They should reach the pueblo within three sleeps, and such a fast would be no great hardship. Yes, it was good. Good to sit in the warm rays of the sun, and breathe clear air, with no odor of human sweat and dung and stale urine. He closed his eyes for a moment. Only a moment, he thought.

He was shocked back to reality by the accusing cry of a magpie. The big black and white bird was perched on a boulder a few paces away, busily sounding a warning. White Fox was stirring, stretching as he awakened from his sleep. Red Feather was alarmed. How long since he closed his eyes?

A quick glance at the sun and the shadows of the rocks showed that it had been only a short while. Still, it was not good. He had been completely oblivious to everything, and that could be a mortal danger. He must be more careful.

"You rest now, Father," White Fox said sleepily.

"No, let us move on," Red Feather answered. "I will sleep later."

He could not have said why, but he felt that they must move. Maybe it was a need to escape an area where he had been caught badly off guard. This spot would remind him of their vulnerability, and he would be uncomfortable until they had left it behind. They rose, walked down the slope to the spring, and drank deeply.

The magpie, satisfied that it had done its duty by repulsing the interlopers, flew off toward the lower slopes. Only a derisive cry over its shoulder reminded Red Feather that he had been guilty of a dangerous lapse of attention. It was fortunate that the bird had startled him awake, and not some real danger.

"Thank you, Little Brother," he muttered quietly after the retreating magpie.

"What did you say, Father?" White Fox asked.

"Nothing. Let us go."

Such an error must not happen again.

19
» » »

They traveled mostly at night. It was too chilly and uncomfortable to rest well anyway. When morning came they would continue on until the warming rays of the sun made it more tolerable to remain inactive. Then one would rest while the other watched. Red Feather did not have another of the worrisome lapses of attention. He did not tell White Fox of the experience, beyond a firm caution to remain alert. He saw the magpie again, once or twice, but only at a distance. At least, it was a magpie, if not the same bird. He had a strong feeling that the bird's raucous cry was a sort of derisive laugh at his ineptness.

White Fox was tolerating the travel well, with the resiliency of youth. He did not complain, even though Red Feather knew that hunger was gnawing at the young man's gut, as it was his own. At least they had no trouble finding water.

The second afternoon when Red Feather awakened, White Fox called his attention to a scrubby growth of pines on a slope a bow shot away. They were gnarled and old-looking, though no taller than a man's head. But the pines were not the boy's prime concern.

"See," he pointed, "the forked tree near the rock on the left."

"Yes, what?"

"There is a squirrel in it."

"But, Fox, we could not kill a squirrel. We have no bow."

"Yes, I know. He would be good to eat, but we cannot catch him. I was watching . . . what does *he* eat?"

They watched the animal as it sat, holding a pine cone in its handlike front paws, and busily gnawing the husk away to get at the seeds.

"Maybe we could eat the seeds too?" the boy suggested.

They rose and walked over to the brushy pines. The squirrel fled, scolding noisily.

"See," Fox pointed, picking up a cone which had been utilized and abandoned. "He has eaten seeds from under these scales."

He selected a fresh cone and began to pry at it.

"Here," suggested Red Feather. "Try a stone."

Clumsily at first, the two placed cones on a flat-topped boulder and chipped away with a stone to expose the small round seeds. Some they crushed accidentally, some were lost in the gravelly soil, but soon their technique improved.

"They taste much like nuts!" White Fox noted.

"Yes," Red Feather agreed. "Slow to gather, but good."

The taste was familiar, and he remembered having eaten such a delicacy with his wife's people.

"Nut-pines!" he said suddenly.

"What?"

"Nut-pines. Your mother's people use these, and that is what the trees are called, in their tongue."

White Fox did not answer. He was staring into the far distance.

"Look!" he said softly, pointing.

A scattered column of riders moved methodically along some sort of trail in the distance. Both of them crouched low in an involuntary attempt to conceal their presence, though there appeared no need. The horsemen were far away. Red Feather watched for a little while, to make certain what he was seeing.

"Who are they? Soldiers?" White Fox asked.

Red Feather braced his elbows on a rock and cupped his hands to make tunnels to look through. Now distant objects would stand out more clearly. He could still not make out individuals or their garments. Colors all appeared the same in the blue of distance. Some things he could tell, however. There must be thirty or forty men, judging from the distance that the party stretched along the trail. They were scattered unevenly, so they were probably not soldiers, who moved in straight lines.

"Not soldiers, I think," he told White Fox.

"Then who? Other Hairfaces!"

"I do not know," Red Feather answered thoughtfully.

The party of riders was moving southwest, in the general direction of Santa Fe. Probably they were following the Southwest Trail, and were coming from the pueblo of Blue Corn's people. Who were they? He remembered the party of rebels who had stopped them on the trail. This appeared to be a larger group, but maybe they had recruited others since . . . how long had it been? It seemed unlikely that this many of the

Spanish who were *not* soldiers would be traveling anywhere, so these must be natives. But what could be the
purpose of such a large group? Uneasily, he remembered Blue Corn's mention of the medicine man Popé,
urging the pueblo people to fight the Hairfaces. Could
it be that general warfare had broken out, or was about
to do so? He wished that he had more information.

Actually, he thought, it made little difference. It
was no great concern to them, except for the danger of
being accidentally caught in the middle. That could be
a danger, of course. But otherwise, let the two sides
settle their differences as they would. The People
would simply stop the trade to Santa Fe until it was
over. He had few friends there anyway, primarily only
Gutierrez. Once more, he wondered why the trader
had not returned to keep him informed. It was not like
Gutierrez. Had something happened to him?

He wished that he had listened to the warnings of
his father-in-law not to go to Santa Fe. But it was no
matter. They had gone, had lost all their possessions,
and had a man killed. But now they were all out of the
city of the Hairfaces. At least, he thought so. They
could start for home. What a comforting thought. Yes,
they would remain neutral, as Blue Corn had. Maybe,
someday, they could resume trading, but for now . . .

"Father, what is going on?" White Fox demanded. "I
do not understand any of this."

"I am not sure I do either, Fox."

"But I thought the Hairfaces were our friends, and
then they put us in the cage. And I do not understand
these others. Are they my mother's people? If they are,
why do we hide from them?"

How to answer the boy? The entire situation had
become so confused, so dangerous.

"Fox," he said slowly, "there is much that we do not know. There is trouble between the Hairfaces and the people of the pueblos."

White Fox nodded.

"But not my mother's people?"

"I think not. Your grandfather has tried to stay out of the trouble. But we do not know for sure. So, we will be careful. When we reach the pueblo, we will start on for home."

"Do you think Turkey Foot and the others will be there?"

"I do not know. Maybe. It does not matter."

"And my mother?"

"Yes, she will be there. If the others have gone on, even, she will stay with her people."

The distant column of riders had now passed out of sight around the shoulder of one of the hills.

"We go on now?" asked White Fox.

Red Feather rose.

"Yes, we go on."

"And we still hide from everyone?"

"Yes, it will be safest. We will still stay out of the trouble."

White Fox did not speak again. His father sighted on a distant peak to establish direction and started off.

It was shortly after dark that they stopped to rest. Night's chill was already making itself felt. White Fox sank to his haunches, leaning back against a rock still warm from the sun. He was quiet for a little while and then chuckled to himself.

"What is it?" asked Red Feather.

"Father," said White Fox, "I do not enjoy trading as much as I thought I would."

20

» » »

They saw no more riders for the rest of the journey. For that matter, they saw no one at all. They seemed to regain some strength as they became more active, and long-unused muscles awoke again to the stimulus of exercise.

Red Feather was reminded somehow of his Vision-Quest. On that occasion, after two days' fasting, the pangs of hunger had left him. There had come over him a calm, clear-thinking feeling. He could see farther, and with a clarity that he had never had before. All his senses were attuned, and he was one with the world.

This journey, after their escape from the foul cell in Santa Fe, was a similar experience. The fresh mountain air and the exercise, in addition to the body changes resulting from the fast, were exhilarating beyond belief. Despite all the concern for the rest of the party, for his wife, and for her people, he was stimulated, his senses honed to a fine edge. He spoke of those things to White Fox, who had also noticed the feeling.

"This is like the Vision-Quest?" the boy asked.

"Yes, much like it. Of course, one sits quietly, and

sleeps and has visions. We do not take the time to do so. We only rest a little and push on.''

They had not taken time to stop again to gather piñon nuts. It was slow work, and gave little results, except perhaps to call attention to their hunger. It was better, Red Feather decided, to keep moving. After all, one must fast or not fast, one could not do both. It was helpful once they stopped teasing the stomach with tiny amounts of food. The hunger pangs ceased.

And in spite of the urgency of their mission, contrasted with the relaxed search of the Vision-Quest, Red Feather found that he did have some sleep-visions. The magpie that had wakened him on that first day returned in his dreams. He was puzzled. The bird was not native to his own prairie country. It was like a new medicine animal, a spirit-guide for this unfamiliar land. The creature in his dreams, however, did or said practically nothing. It was merely there, sounding its scolding cry, as if trying to capture his attention. He puzzled over it, trying to bring meaning, but with little success. He finally decided that it was merely symbolic, that events of importance were happening here in this strange country. He did notice that in each vision the bird flew away to the east. Yes, that must be the significance of the recurrent dream. They must leave the threatening events here, to return east to their more familiar prairie.

Some of his sleep-visions were more sinister. He saw the kind-sad face of the old man who had shared their cell. The old man said nothing, but only looked deeply into his face with dark, sad eyes. Yes, sadness. That was the single most prominent feature of that dream. Sadness, for all the unfortunate misunderstanding that was rampant in the mountain country.

Regret, for all the violence that had occurred, and that would yet do so. It was a detached emotion, an impression by an uninvolved observer. Red Feather woke from the strongest of these dreams with a definite feeling of clarity. The old man was dead. He was certain of it. The detached calm was that of another world.

The other dream was, by contrast, one to stir the blood and cause the heart to race. He relived, again and again, the excitement and terror of the escape. Repeatedly, he climbed through the tiny cell window, afraid that he would be stuck in the opening. Sometimes fear gripped him, the trapped feeling of confinement and of futile attempts to escape, while the earthen walls closed upon him. In all of this was the presence of Never-Speaks, pushing and helping him, lifting from behind.

The death of Never-Speaks was no more real than that of the old man, but it carried more emotion. Red Feather had had an actual part in that. He had been holding the hands of Never-Speaks when the boom of the unseen thunder-stick had ended his life. Red Feather had *felt* it, had felt the spirit cross over. There was none of the calm regret of the other dream, but rather an excited animation, an anticipation of conflict yet unfinished. With all this was a subtle warning of violence and bloodshed yet to come.

He awoke with a start to see White Fox alert and watchful. He was proud of the boy. There beyond, a magpie fluttered from one scrubby tree to another.

This must be the meaning of the visions, he thought. I am being made to see the violence and the sadness that is happening here. The bird signifies our flight back to the prairie of the People. We will leave all of this behind, as soon as possible. It is of no concern to us, if they wish to kill each other. He felt better, now that he thought he had fathomed the meaning of the visions.

He was even more confused, then, when the dreams became stronger and more insistent. Especially, this was true of the magpie. The creature in this dream became more elusive. It was always seen in flight, moving away, and always toward the rising sun. But what other explanation? It *must* symbolize the return to the prairie. What else could it be?

He did not confide his confusion to White Fox. The boy had enough concerns of his own. No, he would wait. There was something missing here, something that had so far escaped his understanding. In time, he felt, it would come to him.

It was also puzzling, however, to find that the feeling of violence in the dream of Never-Speaks became stronger. There was an urgency here, too. He did not understand at all the feeling of impending conflict. If the vision of the magpie was valid, they should be moving *away* from the conflict, not into more bloodshed.

Yet the dreams persisted. It must be, he finally decided, that the visions are twisted. It was not a proper way to seek visions, this frantic activity, the hurried travel with brief rest stops only. That must be it. To see with absolute clarity would require rest and relaxation, in addition to fasting. The enforced activity was blurring the clarity of the visions. He tried to overlook the fact that the dreams were not blurred at all. It was only the interpretation that eluded him.

Finally came the day when he recognized landmarks and felt that it was safe to return to the trail. They could be no more than a day's travel from the pueblo of Blue Corn. They pushed on, with even shorter rest than usual, and toward sunset of the next day approached the cluster of mud lodges.

A couple of children at play looked up in alarm, but then recognized the approaching travelers.

"They are here!" one shouted, racing toward the lodges. "They come!"

Moonflower came to look from the doorway of her father's lodge. There was a moment of disbelief, and she flew down the trail to meet them, into the arms of Red Feather. The two gathered their son into a happy embrace.

Blue Corn stepped from the door and hurried over.

"Where are the others?" he asked.

"What others?" Red Feather answered with another question. "Turkey Foot? Are they not here?"

"No, no," Moonflower said anxiously. "They went to free you. You have not seen them?"

"No! We broke out, and came through the mountains."

The expression on the face of Blue Corn was one of deep concern.

"They went with some of our people," he explained. "They are going to attack Santa Fe."

"*Attack?*" Red Feather blurted in disbelief.

"Yes. They went to try to be sure of your safety when the attack comes."

"But how would they know where to find us?"

"The Señor Gutierrez will show them."

"Gutierrez? *He* is with them?"

"Yes, of course. You did not know?"

Aiee, thought Red Feather. No wonder that the visions are confused. The whole world has gone mad.

21

» » »

Red Feather and his father-in-law talked as the travelers ate. White Fox was oblivious to all but filling his stomach for the first time in many sleeps. He wolfed down astonishing amounts of anything prepared by his mother and grandmother. They, in turn, reveled in the opportunity to feed a hungry youngster.

"But I do not understand about Gutierrez," Red Feather observed.

"Nor do I!" Blue Corn agreed.

"Why was he with them?"

"You know their horses were taken when you were captured?"

"Yes. Gutierrez told me. They had to escape through his back door."

"Ah, I see. Well, they were on foot, and wished to get their horses back. Gutierrez showed them where the horses were kept, and they stole them back."

"Yes, that would be the way of our people," Red Feather agreed.

"They also took most of the other horses."

"Ah, that would make pursuit more difficult," Red

Feather chuckled. "But then, Gutierrez came with them? Why?"

"Of that, I am not sure. It seems he was unhappy with his own people. You know they took his store and all his goods?"

Red Feather had not entirely understood that.

"Whatever the reason," Blue Corn continued, "he left with your men, after they drove off the horses. Maybe he was afraid he would be blamed. But no matter. They happened across some of the followers of Popé, who wanted to kill Gutierrez."

"But why?"

"Because he is a Spaniard. Turkey Foot would not let them do it."

"Tell me, Uncle, it is that bad? They would kill him, only because he is a Hairface?"

"Yes," replied Blue Corn sadly. "It is worse! They nearly fought each other over Gutierrez, your men and those of Popé."

"*Aiee!* What stopped them?"

"Turkey Foot gave them the horses, all but their own. They rode here together. Now they go back to fight in Santa Fe."

"But why did our people go back? It is not their fight."

Blue Corn nodded patiently.

"They wish to free you and Fox, when the others attack. Gutierrez will show them where."

"He is still with them, then?"

"Yes. But now, you are not there."

"So, they will attack for nothing."

He paused to think for a moment.

"It could be very dangerous for them," he observed. "The Spanish will try to kill them because they are with the attackers, but Popé's followers do not trust them because they are outsiders who trade with the Spanish. *Aiee*, both sides will be trying to kill them!"

In addition, he quickly realized, Turkey Foot would be trying to storm the jail near the plaza, in an effort to free the prisoners, who were not even there. That attempt in itself would be extremely dangerous. The thunder-sticks could strike at a distance, from the protection of the thick adobe walls.

"Uncle, I must go and try to stop this."

"You cannot stop it, my son. It has long been gathering."

"No, I mean stop Turkey Foot and the others from attacking the jail. I must go."

"Yes, I know," Blue Corn said sadly. "But it may be too late. They left four . . . no, five sleeps ago."

"Father," said White Fox, "those were the men we saw."

"Yes," mused Red Feather, "they must have been. About forty men?"

The older man nodded.

"But we saw them on the trail, only a day, maybe two, out of Santa Fe. It is already over!"

"No! They were to camp outside of town and wait for the others."

"What others?"

"Ah, Red Feather, you do not understand, yet. Popé intends to have *everyone* help with the attack. They will push *all* the Spanish out of our land, or kill them."

"Your young men are with them?"

He had not, until now, realized that the village was practically empty of men of fighting age.

"Most of them," Blue Corn was saying. "Anyway,

the attack was to wait until everyone from the other pueblos had gathered."

"So it may not have happened yet?"

"Maybe. Maybe not."

"I must go there," Red Feather spoke urgently, rising as he did so. "Maybe I can stop my people. Do you have a horse?"

"We can see. They took nearly every animal. But I will ask. I will go with you."

"And I!" Moonflower interjected. "I just have you back. Now I will not let you go again."

"I think it would be better to go alone," Red Feather said gently. "I can travel fast and light, and maybe reach them before the fighting begins."

Most of the horses at the village had been taken by the young men who had joined the followers of Popé. Blue Corn, however, led the way to an enclosure where a strong-looking dun gelding stood. The animal raised its head and looked at them with large, intelligent eyes.

"Take him," Blue Corn said simply. "He will get you there."

Within a short while, the horse was outfitted with a saddle pad and bridle. Red Feather would not take time to rest, but accepted the bundle of food that Moonflower brought. He held her close for a moment.

"It will all be over soon," he whispered. "Do not worry."

He knew that she would, of course.

"You will go by the Trail?" Blue Corn asked.

"Yes. You think it best, no?"

Blue Corn nodded.

"It will be faster. There should be little danger."

Red Feather slung a borrowed bow and arrows over

his back, and nudged the gelding into an easy lope. He must be careful now. If he rode the horse too hard, it would drop from exhaustion, and he would be on foot. He must pace the journey carefully. Walk or trot at intervals, stop for water and to allow the horse to graze. It would still take two days, at least.

He was still concerned that by the time he arrived, the fighting would have already begun. He was tempted to push on at all costs. No, he told himself, it would not be wise. He smiled at the thought of what his mother would say, that the impulsive side of his nature was due to his father's French upbringing. He must control it, use thought and reason, spare the horse. Not only for the animal's welfare and its value, but for purely sensible reasons. If he lost the horse to fatigue, it might take him another day, or even more, to reach Santa Fe.

After the first lope, to loosen the horse's muscles, he reined in and continued at a fast walk until the animal's breathing steadied. It was growing dark now, and the sun had dropped behind the western mountains. Stars began to appear. He paused to locate the Real-star over his right shoulder. It was unnecessary, because they were following the Trail, but to one from the open prairie, it had become a lifelong habit to verify direction from time to time.

The trail slipped smoothly behind. Twice before dawn he stopped and allowed the horse to rest and graze a little while. The sounds of the night creatures were little different from those of home, he noted. Some different night-bird cries, but the coyote calling to its mate from the distant foothills could have easily spoken from a ridge in the Tallgrass Hills.

Once he was startled by the scream of a great hunting cat, the real-cat of the mountains. Reason told him that it was unlikely to be dangerous, but the sound always made the hairs prickle on the back of his neck. It was like the scream of a woman. The horse was uneasy, too, and Red Feather cut short the rest stop to push on. He had managed to seize a little sleep before the real-cat's cry wakened him.

Later, by daylight, he stopped again to sleep a little while. The horse was hobbled and browsing happily, and Red Feather slept longer than he intended. The days of exhausting travel were overtaking him, his punished body demanding rest.

He heard the horse nicker softly, and came up fighting out of the depths of sleep to rejoin the real world. He was dimly aware that the animal had spoken to another horse, where there should be none. As his eyes focused, he realized that he was surrounded by half a dozen well-armed men. They were wearing the loose-fitting woven shirts of the pueblo people.

"Who are you?" demanded one who appeared to be their leader. "What are you doing here?"

Red Feather sat up, slowly, so as not to spur the strangers into action. The tongue of the newcomers was the same as that of his wife's people, he was pleased to note.

"I am Red Feather, of the Elk-dog People from the plains," he began.

"What are you doing here?"

Aiee, he thought, I have been through this talk before . . . It was far more complicated now. How could he explain that he was hurrying to reach his friends outside of Santa Fe to *prevent* their participation in the hostilities? Things never seemed to become simpler, only more confusing.

"Speak!" demanded the stranger. "And how is it you know our tongue?"

"My wife is of your people," Red Feather answered.

The group seemed to relax a little, except for the leader, who remained suspicious.

"You have not yet answered," the man pointed out. "What are you doing here?"

22

» » »

Red Feather was thinking rapidly. His purpose, his motives, his reason for being here at this time, were all quite complicated. It would be difficult to explain that he had been held in jail, had escaped, but that his friends, who did not know, were planning to rescue him. No, it would be better to simplify the story, even at risk of stretching truth somewhat.

"I am on the way to Santa Fe," he stated calmly.

A militant-looking group such as this must be aware of the coming hostilities, and in all probability were headed there themselves. This thought sparked his next remark.

"Is not everyone?" he asked casually.

The men looked at each other and back to him. Suspicion was strong in their faces.

"*Why* do you go there?" their leader asked.

Red Feather's heart was pounding, his palms sweaty. He hoped they would not notice his uneasiness. He had been suspected before of trading with the Spanish.

"To join my friends, of course. I missed them, back at the pueblo, and they left without me. They are two or three sleeps ahead."

There was still a strong feel of suspicion here. *Aiee*, he thought, I am blamed by both sides for sympathy to the other.

"What are your friends doing in Santa Fe?" someone asked. "Are they of your tribe, or your wife's?"

"Both!" Red Feather said simply. "When the call came from Popé, they left for Santa Fe. I am trying to catch up with them."

"By sleeping?"

"*Aiee*, I have been riding all night, from the lodge of my wife's father, Blue Corn. My horse must rest and graze!"

Some of the men nodded in understanding, and he pushed it a little farther.

"If I ride him to death, I am on foot, no? Then I will not get to Santa Fe in time. And none of us will, if we stand here talking."

There was a chuckle around the circle, and a more relaxed mood.

"Wait . . . you say your wife is the daughter of the Elder, Blue Corn?"

The question was posed by a man who had not spoken before, a small, wiry man with a thoughtful countenance.

"What is your wife's name?" he went on.

"Moonflower. She saved my life once. I was wounded by a thunder-stick and they called Popé himself for the ceremony."

There, that should carry some weight.

There was a gasp from the listeners. He had indeed impressed them.

"It is true," the small, wiry man said. "I have heard this story from my cousin, who lives in that pueblo. This man speaks truth."

"So," Red Feather interjected, "do we go to Santa Fe, or stand and talk?"

There was only a moment of hesitation, and then men began to rein their horses around to start down the trail. Those who had dismounted swung quickly to their seats. Red Feather took the hobbles from his buckskin and mounted.

This had gone rather well, he thought. They had accepted his story. He now had someone with whom to travel, so his position was a little less dangerous in unfamiliar country. Perhaps the best thing about this uneasy alliance was that these men knew of the push against Santa Fe, and were heading there themselves for the attack. This implied that it had not happened yet. He had suggested the idea that they might be too late to participate, but no one had picked up on it. Since this group had more information than he, and were not concerned that they would be late, he would have to assume that it was not quite time for the attack to take place.

The man who appeared to be the leader of this loose-knit group rode up beside Red Feather as they traveled. He was a tall and muscular man. His face had never lost its original expression of hostility since Red Feather had first looked on it. He spoke quietly, so that none heard except Red Feather.

"I am not convinced," the man said evenly. "There is something wrong about you. You do not tell us the whole truth."

Red Feather tried to appear calm and relaxed.

"What more could there be?" he asked innocently.

"I do not know," the other admitted, "but I do not trust you. If you are lying, I will kill you myself."

Once more Red Feather was dismayed at the situation, over which he had less and less control. He was trapped into a series of dangerous events. This man would consider killing him because of a suspicion that he was sympathetic to the Spanish. At the same time, the soldiers would cheerfully kill him because of his association with this group. Not only did this strange double-headed danger threaten him, but every member of the trading party from the plains.

Red Feather tried to chuckle, but it came out wrong, tense and high-pitched. He tried to brave it out.

"My brother," he began insistently, "why would I ride into this kind of danger, if not to fight?"

He could see that the other was not convinced.

"I will be watching," the man growled.

"And how are you called?" asked Red Feather. "I wish to know the name of those who may want to kill me."

"I am Hunting Bear. And I do not believe you know Popé."

"I did not say I know him. He once performed the healing ceremony for me. I was near death at the time, and he was gone when I awoke."

Now Hunting Bear seemed undecided.

"But you did not travel all the way from the plains to fight the Spanish."

"Of course not. We came to trade. We knew nothing of all this."

"So, you *do* trade with the Metal People!"

"Yes, as your people have. Look, your arrows carry iron tips, there is a knife at your waist. Where did those things come from?"

"Yes, your words are true," admitted Hunting Bear.

Red Feather was tempted to go ahead and tell of the

loss of all their furs, and his time in jail, but was reluctant to share all that he knew.

"I still do not trust you. I will be watching," Hunting Bear stated, closing the conversation.

He picked up his reins and kneed his horse ahead.

Red Feather was now thinking deeply about the coming meeting. Hopefully, they would reach Santa Fe before any hostilities began. He could search out Turkey Foot and the others from those assembling for the attack. There should then be no problem for them to leave as a group, to return to Blue Corn, and from there, to start on home.

His worst fears were that the attack would start before this group arrived. Turkey Foot, experienced and wise, but bold and unpredictable, might easily decide to lead the attack on the jail. The men from the plains would be killed needlessly. Further, if the attack was in progress when they arrived, Red Feather would be expected to take an active part in killing Spaniards, under the watchful eye of Hunting Bear.

There seemed no way out, except to continue hoping that they would reach Santa Fe in time. They were traveling much more slowly than he had intended, and he chafed at the delay. Continually, he attempted to hurry their progress a little. As easygoing and unaware of the passage of time as his own people were, these men were frustrating beyond belief. Maybe, he thought, it is as my mother says. I have inherited impatience from my father.

But, he answered his own thought, there is a reason for impatience here. One not known to the others of this party, and one he could not share with them, or make them understand. He nudged the dun just a trifle, trying to hurry the pace without seeming to do so. He estimated that night that they would reach Santa Fe not tomorrow, but by the middle of the next day.

He hoped that would be soon enough.

23

» » »

Gutierrez sat alone near the camp, frustrated and worried. The group had encountered others as they traveled, and numbers had increased. Only now was he beginning to realize that this was big, an all-out rebellion. And here he was, trapped, caught up in the gigantic sweep of events.

It no longer bothered him that any newcomer looked on him with dark glances of suspicion. Turkey Foot and the others had been careful to explain his presence. It helped also that he was wearing the native shirt of rough-woven wool, rather than his usual clothing. He was far less conspicuous. It was also true that as the camp enlarged, with newcomers every day, more men were strangers to each other. Anyone's mere presence here implied loyalty to the cause.

They had been told on arrival, less than a day outside Santa Fe, that Popé would come soon. Rumors circulated constantly. The attack, it was said, would come in three or four days. Then two. No, three. No one actually knew, but it was plain that they must wait for word, and then begin the attack.

Gutierrez had been confronted with serious trouble

on the day after they arrived. He conceived the idea that he might go into town, check on the condition of Red Feather and White Fox, and tell them to expect rescue. He might also tell María what was afoot, and that he would rejoin her soon. He would not actually take part in the fighting, but would show the way to the jail for the rescue of Red Feather and then withdraw to the safety of noncombatant status.

When he mentioned this plan to Turkey Foot, he was met with doubts, then with a flat refusal, as the others in the party learned of the plan.

"We cannot let you do this," one of the pueblo leaders told him threateningly.

"But I must tell our friend to expect rescue," he protested.

"No. You will warn the Hairfaces."

"No, no. You have my promise!"

The other shook his head.

"Your promise is not good. You will not even come back."

Gutierrez was offended.

"My word is good!" he insisted. "I am known to your people for many seasons. Ask those who know me!"

"But I do not know you," the other man declared, "and I do not trust you. This is too important, and we will kill you if you try to go into town."

Turkey Foot came to his defense.

"He can be trusted," he pointed out. "We have traded with this man for many summers. We need to tell our friend in jail to expect us!"

"No!" snapped the man from the pueblos. "I do not really trust you, either! You have traded with our enemies. We only let you come with us to help your friend. But you must do as we say."

Now Turkey Foot, too, was frustrated. He conferred with the others from the plains.

"We will do nothing but free Red Feather," he pointed out. "Then we leave. Let us stay close together, all of us. This will not be our fight."

So the few days dragged past. The entire camp was restless and irritable, impatient for action. Gutierrez knew that he was watched, and fidgeted under the observation that he felt. He had given up on the idea of attempting to slip away to town. His fear would not let him take the risk. In sheer frustration he would walk a little way out of camp and merely sit, to be alone. He was careful to remain in plain sight, because he did not want anyone to misunderstand his motives.

It was during one of these private interludes that another idea occurred to him. He might be of use in avoiding bloodshed. His entire career as a trader involved negotiation. There was always a give-and-take, a need to see the position of the other side. And in this case, he could see that there were injustices. If he had a chance, maybe he could start some negotiation here. He was sympathetic to some of the natives' grievances, though loyal to his own people. That could be an advantage. Yes, he told himself, maybe he could be a hero here, if he could manage to deter the hostilities. But he must have help.

Turkey Foot was again quite dubious.

"They will not let you go in," he reminded Gutierrez. "They told you that."

"But this is different," Gutierrez insisted. "I would go in just before the attack."

"That would be too late."

Probably, Gutierrez agreed, but what would be lost? He could go straight to the military authorities, who by that time would realize the overwhelming size of the onslaught. He would offer to negotiate, using his chance contacts with the natives.

Turkey Foot shook his head.

"The Hairfaces would not do it."

"But they could do no more than say no."

"That is true," Turkey Foot agreed. "It could do no harm, if they already know of the attack."

"Besides," Gutierrez pressed, "it would be of help if we could go in before the attack. I could show you where Red Feather is held."

It was that point which finally convinced Turkey Foot.

"It is good," he agreed, "but we must talk to the pueblo men. They have forbidden you to go in."

Again, they met a stone wall of resistance.

"No," was the flat answer. "The time for talk is past."

"But, señor," pleaded Gutierrez, "what harm can it do? They will already know of the coming attack."

"Popé will not meet with them," insisted the other man.

"I do not know if they would meet with him," Gutierrez insisted, "but it is of no cost to try."

Gutierrez' success as a trader was no coincidence. He was a very persuasive man, and from long practice could read others' feelings expertly. Now he saw a slight indecision on the swarthy face.

"If they do not agree, nothing is lost," he reminded.

"Well," said the pueblo man cautiously, "we would not wait for you. We attack anyway, unless they come out to talk first."

"Agreed."

It was a long shot, Gutierrez thought, but he must try.

"It is good," observed Turkey Foot. "Swallow and I will go in with you. That will put us with Red Feather before the attack comes."

Gutierrez could see that the old man still had grave doubts, but was willing to use the situation to free Red Feather. Gutierrez felt somewhat better, now that there was at least some sort of direction in his immediate future.

It was just before dark that same evening that word spread with the rapidity of a prairie fire. The attack was to be at sunrise.

"You can go in just ahead," offered the pueblo sub-chief with whom they had talked. "I have told the others to let you go."

Gutierrez was distressed. He would have little time, and in the early morning the senses would be dull. He began to wonder if this was a senseless effort. No matter, he concluded. He must do it now.

Excitement pervaded the camp as everyone checked his weapons and prepared to leave. Turkey Foot called his party together to speak to them. He looked them over in the gathering dusk. Yellow Robe, Swallow, Broken Lance, and his sister's son, Bull's Horn. Strong young men. He wondered how many would go home this year. Already they had lost Red Dog.

"We stay together," he reminded. "Swallow and I go in first, with the trader. Then, when you come in, we meet you in the plaza. We will have Red Feather with us, or we will free him together. Remember, this is not our fight, unless we must, to defend ourselves."

It was a long speech for Turkey Foot, but necessary.

"What if we are separated?" asked Yellow Robe.

Turkey Foot thought for a moment.

"We meet back here," he decided. "Near that big rock that looks like a bear sitting down. If any are missing, we wait until the next morning and then go home."

The others nodded, and turned back to preparing for travel. Gutierrez already felt his heart racing, and his palms were beginning to sweat. How had he ever become involved in this?

24

» » »

Blue Corn walked along the stream as he loved to do, alone in his thoughts. This morning, however, he was deeply troubled. As happy as they had been to see their daughter and her family, he wished that they had not come.

The country was seething with trouble. It was bad, and he was certain that things would be worse before they were better. He had tried to warn Red Feather, but one could go only so far in imposing on the choice of another.

Ah, yes, he reflected, there lay one of the major causes of trouble. He did not understand the urgency that seemed to push the Hairface elders. They had a good story to tell, there was no doubt. One of the finest creation stories he had ever heard. But why did they refuse to listen to any story but theirs? In the past few seasons, they had become more and more insistent. They had imprisoned and killed or maimed a number of the Elders of the pueblos. Especially in towns to the west, he had heard, the punishment had been severe. Hands or feet had been chopped off as punishment for such things as performing traditional ceremonies. And, of course, the most horrifying of all, the death by the rope.

Why? To Blue Corn's people, it was ludicrous to tell another what he must think. A person believes what his heart tells him, he mused.

He walked thoughtfully to sit on the silver-gray trunk of the dead cottonwood, where he could think, alone. He had feared for the life of his daughter's husband. They had been happy for their daughter, that she and her family were far away on the plains, away from the danger that lurked in the pueblos and the kivas. So it had been with some degree of distress that they had welcomed Moonflower home. Blue Corn had wished a speedy conclusion to the trading venture, so that Moonflower, her family, and the others could return to the plains, before disaster could strike. Instead, Red Feather had alighted squarely in the midst of the trouble. It had been fortunate, Blue Corn thought, that only one of the men from the plains had been killed.

Only one, so far. The situation now looked quite menacing. Turkey Foot and the others had gone back to free Red Feather, not knowing that he was already free. Blue Corn had considered going with them. He would have done so, except that he was afraid that his age and infirmities would be a burden. The rescue party must be more quick and mobile than the stiffness of his old limbs would allow. No, he must leave it to the younger men.

He devoutly hoped that Red Feather would be able to overtake the others before the hostilities started. That would solve the problems rather nicely. The men from the plains would simply turn around and start back, away from the danger.

Blue Corn caught a glimpse of motion along the stream, and looked up to identify the approaching woman. It was Moonflower. She came and sat beside him on the log. Both were silent for a little while, merely sharing companionship in their concern.

"Your son is doing well?" he asked finally.

She smiled.

"Yes, he is stronger each day. With each bite, almost. *Aiee*, I have never seen one eat so! But yes, he recovers quickly. He seems to have forgotten."

"One never forgets such a thing," Blue Corn observed, "but he has overcome it well. He is a fine son, Moonflower."

"Like his father," she agreed, pleased at the compliment.

Then she became serious.

"Father, do you think Red Feather will find them?"

"Of course," he said quickly.

Then he paused. He could not deceive her.

"He will find them," he went on sympathetically, "but this concerns me, too. Will he find them in time to avoid the fighting? Maybe so, maybe not."

"What will happen, Father?"

"To them?"

"No, to us all. To you and Mother, to the pueblo here. Are these really bad times?"

He was quiet for a little while. There were many among his people who saw this as only a temporary thing, this trouble. He had long suspected that it was more. It was odd that his daughter, who had been away for many years, could feel it, too. The Spanish had been here for many generations, for more than a hundred summers. No one now alive could remember when it was otherwise. But now, there was a feeling of finality, of an end of an era. No matter what happened in Santa Fe, things would never again be the same. He viewed this with a feeling of immense sadness and regret. Now it seemed that Moonflower was also feeling such a finality. She had always been perceptive. It was her keen spirit that had saved the dying youth who would become her husband. How short a time ago that seemed, though it was now half a lifetime.

"Father?" Moonflower queried.

"What? Oh yes, I was lost in my thoughts. Such is the privilege of age."

He took a deep breath.

"Ah, yes. You had asked, what will happen? I do not know, my daughter. Your husband will have his friends to help him. He knows that you and White Fox are safe, here, and that, too, will help him."

"But, I . . ."

"Yes, yes, I know, that is not your question. Your spirit is keen, my daughter. You see, as I do, that these are times of great change. It will never be the same again."

"The same as when I was small?" she asked.

"Or when I was small," he said thoughtfully. "Maybe this is the end of our people."

"Father!" she blurted.

She had never heard him talk so.

"Times change," he observed. "I do not know how it was before the Hairfaces came, long ago. But it must have been different, with no metal knives or tools. Even so, with all that they have brought, good and bad, there are changes now not seen before."

"What do you mean?"

"It is hard to think about. I . . . well, look. Never before have our Elders urged the killing of those who are not of our people. We have had few enemies, through all of the long-ago times."

"But now it is different?"

Moonflower did not understand what he was trying to say.

"Yes," he said slowly, "what will happen when Popé arrives from Taos? He is not going to Santa Fe to talk. There will be much bloodshed. What will this do to our people? We have always been a people of peace. Even if Popé succeeds in driving out the Metal People, it will be with much killing. Can our people ever be the same again?"

Putting it into words was helping Blue Corn to understand what it was that concerned him. Would the very means of attempting to return to the old ways be the destruction of tradition? He feared that here was an impossible task before them. In order to maintain the ancient traditions of peaceful existence, they would make war. Would that not, in itself, destroy that which they hoped to save? He saw no way out of the trap.

"We can only wait and see," he concluded, "and this is not easy."

He looked up and down the stream. It looked much the same as it had when he was a boy, and had played along its banks. It spoke the same murmuring language that it had then. Other generations of children might play here, in the shade of cottonwoods now small, but which would someday be great trees like the dead giant on which they sat. The cottonwoods sprouted, grew, and died, though their generation was much longer than that of a man. The stream was a thing of more permanence.

There was something here that eluded him, an idea

that was trying to make itself felt. It had something to do with the cottonwoods. He looked at the small tree beside the trunk of the dead giant. It was making a new start for its kind. That, somehow, was what would be necessary. After the hostilities were over, someone must begin anew, to make a new start.

But what kind of a start? On this, he was as confused as ever. How could his people start over?

Even more important to his family on this day, what was happening in Santa Fe, or on the trail from Taos?

25

》》》

The air fairly crackled with excitement as the men of the pueblos moved into position around the town. It would not be a disciplined attack. Even Gutierrez, with his lack of military experience, could see that. The only thing in common was the cause which brought these men together. The tradition of the leaders as merely "first among equals" was still strong.

It was a departure from tradition, then, for a leader to arise in the kivas. The charismatic Popé brought a mystical message that urged actions unheard of in the tradition of these people. They were carried along on the great strength of his spirit.

"Popé is here!"

The rumor spread like a forest fire through the waiting warriors. The knowledge of the presence of the leader was in itself almost a mystical experience. There was still no major organization, but the charisma of the famous Elder brought a spiritual kinship to each man.

Turkey Foot was concerned for the safety of Gutierrez, as well as their own. He had tried to make certain that everyone along this particular area of the attack was aware of their presence. If the pueblo men knew of outsiders in their company, they would show more restraint when selecting targets for their arrows. The different dress of the men from the plains would not be much of a problem. It could still be plainly seen that they were natives, not Spanish.

Regarding Gutierrez, Turkey Foot was more concerned. The man *looked* like a Spaniard. In the heat of battle . . . *aiee*, it might be a problem. There would be large numbers, maybe hundreds, of warriors anxious to kill the hated Hairfaces, and who were not aware of the trader's friendship. He and Swallow must stay close to protect the trader.

Turkey Foot's hope was that they could enter the town ahead of the others, locate and free Red Feather and Fox, and be gone before the attack really began. They could help Gutierrez make contact with his own people, where he would find relative safety. As much safety as anyone would on this day. Turkey Foot had a bad feeling for it. He hoped he was wrong, because he knew there was nothing else that they could do. They must try to help Red Feather, as well as Gutierrez, who had long been their friend.

He did not relish the prospect of a fight, as he once had. The stress of many winters had taken its toll. He had noticed, the past few seasons, how Cold Maker would take opportunity to stiffen his joints and make his limbs ache when the winds of autumn turned to the north. Even in summer, the chill of a mountain night made itself felt in his aging bones. It was not bad this morning. He had not slept, for the immobility of sleep would have made the stiffness worse. Still, he did not relish the prospect of battle.

As a young man, he had distinguished himself in

the few battles that had involved his people. Largely, his had been a lifetime of peace, but there was the year when they had been forced into a confrontation with a village of Mandans. It had been settled with only a few skirmishes, with dignity to both sides. He himself had fought well, had killed men, and had counted many honors. There were none who could question his courage. But today was different. He had no clear-cut quarrel with any here, except those who had seized their furs. He still regarded the whole thing as some sort of misunderstanding. Through the years, they had always paid a tribute to those in power. Sky-Eyes had said that among the Hairfaces it was the accepted way. It had always proved so, until this year.

Ah, well, no matter. By noon, they would have Gutierrez back among his people, and would have freed Red Feather. Then they would be on the trail again, free from all the worry of who will do what. That would be good. He tried to ignore the nagging concern that continued to nudge at him, the sense of impending tragedy. To put himself in the proper mood and lift himself above such concerns, he silently repeated the Death Song of the people from the plains:

> "The grass and the sky go on
> forever,
> But today is a good day
> to die . . ."

Gutierrez was tying a white rag to a stick. Turkey Foot saw in the dim predawn light that it was a scrap of the trader's shirt, the one he had worn on the night they had stolen the horses. Gutierrez now wore the native shirt given him by Blue Corn. That would be good, Turkey Foot reflected. There would be less chance of misidentification. But what of this rag?

"What are you doing?" he asked.

Gutierrez looked up and smiled, his teeth gleaming white.

"It is the way of the Spanish, as well as others," he explained. "This white flag says I would talk, not fight."

"It is a signal?"

"Yes. I will talk to them. Maybe they will talk to this Popé, settle their differences."

Turkey Foot listened to the dull hum of voices along the slope. He had doubts that it would be possible to stop the forces now already in motion. It was like that time with the Mandans. It had been necessary to fight to establish the right of his people and their allies to camp on the river and to hunt where the buffalo were found. After that, there was no problem. They had traded peaceably for the rest of the summer. Many robes, much dried meat had changed hands. Some of the men had even taken Mandan wives. He could understand that Gutierrez would want to talk peace, but had grave doubts that it would work.

Anyway, he and Swallow would accompany the trader into town to try. It was a good idea, he reflected, the peace sign of the Hairfaces. If they refused to talk, there was no harm done. Gutierrez could stay there, after showing them where to find Red Feather. Maybe he and Swallow would withdraw, to return with the attackers and open the cage.

Then why, he wondered, did he have bad feelings for the day?

It was growing a little lighter now, and the warriors

were growing more impatient. They must make their move.

"We go now," he told the group of pueblo men near them.

The others nodded assent. Turkey Foot swung up to the back of his horse.

"You *ride* in?" someone asked.

Turkey Foot had not really considered anything else. In the minds of the people from the plains, "a man on foot is no man at all." It now occurred to him that in the close fighting that would come among the mud lodges of the town, to be on foot would be a great advantage. He must change his thinking, but there was no time.

"We go in to talk, not fight," he explained. "The white flag of the trader is medicine to protect us. We can dismount when the fighting comes."

Turkey Foot, Swallow, and Gutierrez now urged their horses forward at a walk. Gutierrez had expressed doubts as to the wisdom of riding in, also. He would have been more comfortable on foot, but Turkey Foot insisted. The proper way to approach a council, in his mind, was to do so sitting tall and proud on a horse. Besides, if the white flag acted as Gutierrez said, this would be an advantage. The flag could be seen more easily in the dim light.

They rode toward the town, Gutierrez looking nervous but proud between the two men from the plains. At the end of his stick fluttered the scrap of white shirt that would guarantee their safety.

At least, Turkey Foot devoutly hoped that it would. He could not overcome the bad feeling that he had for this day.

26

》》》

In all probability, Manuel Ruiz was a misfit to begin
with. He had never done anything that particularly
distinguished him from the crowd, but then neither
had any of his family. Nor, had anyone that he knew.
Actually, it was better to blend into the crowd, Manuel always felt. If no one notices you, pays you no
attention, that is good. If you are noticed, the attention you reap is usually unpleasant, he had observed.
At any rate, it was true in his experience.

His military career had borne out this theory. Do a
good enough job to get by, but not too good so that
you are noticed, for then you will be watched. It had
been so at home, where he was one of nine children.
Those who distinguished themselves from the others,
either good or bad, drew the wrath of their father.
That was something greatly to be avoided. He had run
away at the age of sixteen to join the army. Maybe it
was fifteen, for his mother had not kept count very
well. Maybe it was his brother Jesus who was sixteen.
But it mattered little. Manuel was soon in uniform,
serving the Crown.

It was ideal, the life of a soldier. His uniform made

him attractive to the women. At least, there was always somebody to help him spend a few pesos of his
pay. He ate more regularly, and his stomach, which
had always seemed empty during his childhood, was
now often comfortably full. Despite this, it did not
seem to stick to his ribs. Maybe it was the lasting effect
of his early years, but Manuel remained as scrawny as
ever. He was lanky of frame, though not tall, and even
the best-fitting uniform hung loosely on his spare
shoulders.

The hair of his beard, too, grew sparsely and in un-
even bunches, like the bunch grass of the sun-baked
deserts of New Spain. Mother of God, how he hated it.
Not the beard. He could do something about that. He
could shave it occasionally or let it grow, depending
on how much pressure he was receiving from immediate superiors. He would do what was necessary to appear as nearly like everyone else as he could. The
uniform certainly helped. He could be one of the face-
less mass of soldiers, just another in the ranks, able to
disappear in the crowd at the slightest threat of work
or responsibility.

His basically lazy, low-key style had helped, too. All
in all, the army had been good for him. Though he was
a misfit, he could go unnoticed as he practiced the few
skills he had perfected. Useful skills for a soldier, they
were: the ability to remain inconspicuous, to avoid
work wherever possible, and an uncanny sense of
when to be difficult to find.

This assignment at Santa Fe was not bad duty. He
had detested some of the posts farther south, dry,
sandy places without shade and with no apparent re-
deeming features. This was somewhat better. The
mountainous climate was to his liking. True, it was

hot in the daytime, but one could usually find shade. And in the evening, it became comfortable, as the gentle night breezes came cooling down the slopes to refresh the sun-baked town.

There were two things that rankled him tonight, however. One was the tense uneasiness that gripped the place. Manuel did not know, or care, what it was all about. It had all started a hundred years ago, somebody said, when Spain first came to bring the Crown and the Cross to the savages. There had always been some resistance to Christianity, it was said. He did not understand that. It was easy to go to Mass, and to say confession as the priests wished. Not too much of a confession, of course. That would be self-defeating, as it would draw attention, and that in turn would violate his basic principles of invisibility. No, he would merely confess enough to please the priest, thus drawing no attention to himself. He did not understand why this was not the pattern followed by the savages. It would have avoided trouble for them. But there were some, it was said, who were not content to let things slide along without effort. Some of the natives had begun to defy the priests. They would hold their own savage rituals in the villages.

Manuel resented this bitterly. Not the rituals, or even the defiance, but the fact that it was interfering with his own well-ordered life. Here he was, finally, for the first time ever, in a relatively pleasant place. He had gained a well-balanced anonymity, was hardly noticed by those in authority, and had plenty to eat. Now these cursed savages had to mess it all up with their stupid defiance of the priests' demands. Why couldn't they let it alone?

The savages were also responsible for his other discomfiture tonight. He had been chosen for sentry duty. It was not always possible to avoid such things, to be sure, but he would not have been picked tonight except for the gathering clouds of conflict. Double sentries were posted because of anticipated trouble, and Manuel was trapped. He had managed to avoid the watch on the first round, but with double duty it was inevitable. He had drawn the midnight to dawn watch at the northeast edge of the town.

Now he stood, leaning in the shadows against the adobe wall of one of the last structures at the edge of the town. He was restless, uneasy, and a little bit frightened. He could sense activity in the foothills. It was known that there was a large gathering of natives in the mountains. Their fires could be seen at night, if one cared to go and look. Manuel did not care to do so. It violated his policy of not seeking trouble. No one knew exactly what was happening, but *something* seemed imminent. For a large gathering of natives, there must be a purpose. Manuel Ruiz did not know what it might be, but he was keenly aware that the dragoons had stopped their mountain patrols because of the danger of ambush.

Now he gripped his matchlock musket with sweating palms and peered into the predawn darkness. Yes, he was sure of it now. There was motion out there. Large numbers of people were moving around somewhere. He could hear the soft mutter of sound from a thousand unshod hooves. Or maybe, even, moccasined feet. There was a crawling sensation at the back of his neck.

If he could hold out a little longer, he would be off duty. If, of course, that damned Lopez came to relieve him on time. Manuel chose to ignore the fact that he himself had been late in relieving Ortega. Should he go and report his observations to the corporal of the guard? No, he decided. He actually had nothing to report. It would seem quite stupid in the light of day to have reported noises in the dark.

Possibly his major reason for not doing so, however, was his basic tenet of not drawing attention to himself. Let one of the other sentries be the one who made the report.

It was beginning to yellow a little in the east, and Manuel smiled. He was going to make it through his watch now, and would soon be seeking his blankets. Then, in the still uncertain light, he realized that he could not only feel and hear the motion in the hills, he could *see* it. Men were moving, in a slow and systematic approach to the town. He had no idea how many, but the numbers were large. He froze for an instant, but then realized that he must do something.

He looked down at his musket. It had never made much difference to him that his unit was armed with the old-style matchlock guns, until now. How he wished at this moment for a modern flint-fire weapon. As it was, he would have to ignite his match.

Quickly, Manuel stepped around the corner of the building and knelt to draw out his flint and steel. With shaking hands he unwrapped the rag from around the breech of the weapon and felt the cord of the match. It seemed dry. Good. The saltpeter with which the cord was impregnated had not drawn too much moisture from the night air.

Even so, it seemed that he struck a dozen or more sparks before one caught on the tip of the match and it began to smolder. The acrid smoke of the burning salt peter made him sneeze as he jumped to his feet and peered around the corner again.

It was lighter now. He could plainly see the individual forms flitting silently from rock to bush on the hillside. But even nearer, three horsemen rode toward him. They came slowly, and appeared to be peaceably inclined. Still, as a precaution, Manuel leveled his musket and sighted along the barrel.

The two men on either side were clearly natives. Manuel had never bothered to learn the differences in natives. They were all savages anyway, and they all looked alike. The man in the middle, however, appeared different. He sat his horse a bit awkwardly, possibly because he was a bit fatter than the others. He carried a stick, at the top of which a white rag fluttered. Manuel was confused. Was this an offer to talk? Who was this man?

In the growing light, Manuel began to notice other things. The man looked *Spanish!* He was wearing boots and Spanish trousers, but one of the loose woolen shirts of the savages, belted at the waist. A traitor? It certainly seemed so.

Somehow, all of the frustrations of Manuel's unsatisfactory life began to boil to the surface. All of his current problems, all the unease of a potentially dangerous situation, seemed to come forward and center on this man. If it had not been for him, Manuel found himself thinking, this would still be pleasant duty, and Manuel Ruiz would be back in his blankets.

The three were within easy range now. Manuel slid the cover off the musket's priming pan. He would shoot, not at the man, but just to sound the alarm. He sighted at the fluttering flag for a moment, and then experimentally lowered the barrel a little, to center on the man's chest. It would be so easy . . . he could deny that he had fired the shot, or claim a misfire. The outmoded matchlock muskets were known for erratic behavior.

With hardly a conscious thought, Manuel's finger seemed to tighten on the trigger lever. The smoldering match dropped into the priming powder. There was a flash, and a heartbeat later the main charge boomed.

The man on the horse was knocked backward as if swatted by a giant hand. The white rag fluttered to the ground, and the horse danced nervously, frightened without a guiding hand on the rein. Before the limp form struck the dirt, however, Manuel Ruiz was running, terrified and breathless, toward the center of town. Behind him, there was one long, blood-curdling yell, which almost made him stumble in its intensity. He did not see how such a sound could come from a human throat.

In truth, it was not a sound familiar to these mountains. Its proper home was far to the northeast. It was a challenge, a defiant threat and a promise of vengeance, voiced by two throats in unison. It was a mixture of the yipping challenge of the Head Splitters and the deeper, full-throated war cry of the People from the prairie.

27

》 》 》

Turkey Foot and Swallow stared for an instant in disbelief as their companion was struck down without warning.

"There he goes!" cried Swallow, pointing to the retreating soldier.

He spurred forward in pursuit.

"Wait!" called Turkey Foot. "There may be more!"

Swallow reined his horse around, turning the excited animal in a tight circle. It was a hard decision, not to fight back when attacked, but the danger was obvious. One does not ride headlong into the unknown.

Turkey Foot had dismounted to examine the fallen Gutierrez. The trader was beyond help, his eyes staring sightlessly at the sky. There was still a look of surprise on his face, and in the center of his forehead was a round blue hole which oozed dark blood from its edges. Turkey Foot swung back to his horse in one smooth motion. From his throat came the yipping, defiant war cry of his people. It was joined by the full-throated yell of Swallow as he came pounding back.

Gutierrez' horse was dancing skittishly, rolling

white-rimmed eyes at the figure on the ground. When the double-throated war cry reverberated along the street, the animal panicked completely. It reared high, stepped on a rein, jerked loose, and fled back the way they had come.

The two riders followed at a quick lope, aware now of a stirring-awake in the town behind them. There could be pursuit at any moment. They thundered out of town and along the road until they were aware of the mass of moving humanity ahead of them in the growing light. They reined in as they approached.

"What happened?" someone called.

"The trader is dead!" answered Swallow.

"They killed him? His own people killed him?"

"It is so," Turkey Foot stated.

"Would they not talk to him?"

"He did not have a chance to ask. They killed him without a word," Swallow declared, incredulously.

"His own people killed him?"

"Yes, yes, he lies in the street, there!" Turkey Foot insisted. "A soldier shot him with a smoke stick."

"Killed him . . . his own people . . ."

The murmur went through the crowd. Even those who were not acquainted with the trader became indignant.

"Who? . . . the trader . . . the Hairfaces killed him . . . one of their own!"

The sun was peeping over the earth's rim, and the men began to move forward. There were shouts up and down the ragged line. There was no reason for silence now. They had been discovered. Most of the men were on foot, and the men from the plains, realizing the advantage, dismounted. A few boys had been designated to herd the horses, and Turkey Foot's party turned the animals over to their care.

"Stay together," Turkey Foot called. "We still must free Red Feather."

"Did you learn where he is?" one of the others asked.

"No, we did not have time. But the lodge with the man-cages must be near the plaza. We will go there."

Someone called out and pointed ahead. A column of dragoons was clattering down the street at a trot. Apparently the soldiers had managed to recover enough horses to mount a squad. Even as they watched, the officer in front yelled a command and drew his saber. The others followed the command and their long lances swung into position, shiny points lowered for the charge.

Some of the advancing warriors hesitated, but only for a moment. They scattered among the adobe buildings to take up positions for combat.

The soldiers quickened their pace to a trot, then a full canter, and came charging down the street. An arrow or two arched through the air and fell short.

"Wait!" Turkey Foot called to his party. "Let them come closer."

It was frightening to see the massed strength of the dragoons bearing down on them. With difficulty they refrained from shooting. Turkey Foot was pleased to see that his young men remained calm. Young and inexperienced warriors sometimes panicked in their first battle. He waited, his arrow fitted to the bowstring, carefully choosing his target. It would be the officer in front, he decided. It was always best to try to put down the leader of the enemy. This chief did not appear dangerous as a fighter, but he was in command.

Turkey Foot had always thought it strange that the chiefs and sub-chiefs of the Hairfaces were chosen not for ability but by appointment. Thus the Hairface warriors sometimes had good chiefs, sometimes poor ones. It was a strange way to do things.

The troopers thundered past the still form of Gutierrez in the street, and swept down on the partially hidden men behind houses, walls, and trees. Now arrows began to fly. A horse screamed in pain and began to buck uncontrollably, unseating the rider. A soldier fell, then another, wounded or dead from the thickening rain of arrows.

Turkey Foot took careful aim at the center of the officer's blue tunic, just where the white belts crossed diagonally, and released his arrow. He could tell, even as the string left his fingers, that his shot was wide. There was too much confusion, and his reflexes were slower than in his youth. He fitted another arrow. The officer was more capable than he appeared, Turkey Foot thought. He was a brave man, riding through the hail of arrows to lead his soldiers. Before Turkey Foot could loose his second shot, someone else's arrow struck the man and he fell heavily. His foot caught in the stirrup, and the terrified horse came pounding past, dragging the helpless rider. If he was not already dead, he soon would be, Turkey Foot reflected. He loosed an arrow at another target, and saw it find its mark. His confidence returned.

The troopers were now among the attackers, searching for targets for their lances. A warrior fell, dying, skewered by a fortuitous thrust. Hardly had the lancer finished his withdrawal, though, than he, too, joined his victim in the dust.

A sergeant, wielding a saber, was dealing some telling strokes. Turkey Foot saw a warrior struck by the flashing blade across his shoulder. He fell, rose again, and retreated, his left arm flopping helplessly while blood gushed from his wound. Then the sergeant himself was pulled from his horse by several reaching hands, pounded into the dust, and hacked to pieces with his own saber.

A lancer rushed toward Turkey Foot at a full charge. There was no time to fit another arrow, so he reached for the small ax at his waist. It was a quick throw, but successful. The weapon struck the trooper full in the face, and Turkey Foot stepped aside while the horse thundered past and the lance fell from a lifeless hand. He turned to pursue the stricken trooper and retrieve his ax.

In a surprisingly short time, it was all over. A few surviving troopers, now leaderless, were retreating toward the center of town. A yell of victory rose from the warriors in the street.

Turkey Foot looked quickly around for the others of his party. Swallow's buckskin sleeve was ripped and bloody, but everyone else appeared unharmed.

"Are you . . ." Turkey Foot began.

"It is nothing," Swallow assured them. "A scratch!"

"Come, then," Turkey Foot beckoned. "We will find Red Feather."

Some of the other men were stripping parts of uniforms from the corpses for trophies, and some were wildly hacking and mutilating. Such a frenzy appeared unusual and out of character for the normally tolerant people of the pueblos. Turkey Foot found it difficult to understand. Among his own people, warfare was a long tradition, but here . . . ah, well, no matter, they must go and find Red Feather.

He led the way past the still form of Gutierrez and on toward the center of town.

"He was a brave man," one of the others said as he passed. "We must mourn him."

"Yes," agreed Turkey Foot, "but not now. I am made to think that this fight is just beginning."

As if to confirm the observation, there was the distant boom of a musket from another part of town. It was followed by a roar of excited yells from a hundred throats as attackers pressed forward on a different sector.

"Come," Turkey Foot urged, "while they are fighting there, we will find Red Feather."

28
» » »

It was near dawn on the day of the battle when Red Feather and the pueblo men neared Santa Fe. They had ridden all night.

The evening before, while they were preparing to camp, a traveler had approached with news. Popé was coming. He had left Taos already, and the attack would be next morning at sunrise. They broke camp quickly and pushed ahead to reach Santa Fe before dawn.

Red Feather's motives were different, of course, from those of his companions. The others were anxious to take part in the assault against the hated Spanish. Red Feather, on the other hand, wished to prevent the participation of Turkey Foot and the men of the plains. They would take any risk necessary to find and free him, he was sure. They still believed him to be a prisoner. He must reach them, must stop them before they rushed into a foolhardy, heroic charge, risking life in a completely useless effort.

He did not know what to expect, and had no way of guessing whether they would reach Santa Fe in time. As the night wore on, he began to glance back over his shoulder at the eastern sky. Each time he looked, he feared to see the muddy yellow smudge along earth's rim, which would herald the return of Sun Boy. Each time he saw only the black dome of sky, dotted with sparkling points of light.

Then came the time when he turned, and yes, there it was. A pale, scarcely perceptible thinning of the darkness along the line where earth meets sky. The stars shone with less brilliance against this paling sky. Moreover, he could almost see the dawn grow with each instant.

There was a shout from ahead, and the party reined in. He could hear the nervous stamp of horses somewhere in the darkness to the front. Someone had caused them to stop. There was animated conversation and Hunting Bear came riding back.

"They have already gone in," he announced, seen dimly in the thinning darkness. "The attack is at sunrise."

The riders started to push on, but one of the horse handlers spoke.

"You will leave the horses here?"

"Did the others do so?" Hunting Bear asked.

"Yes. They thought it better to fight on foot."

Red Feather and the other new arrivals began to step down, release their horses, and ready their weapons. It was possible now to see each other, as the morning began to open.

There was a distant boom, which reverberated along the foothills and came echoing back, again and yet once more before it shattered on the peaks and died. Red Feather paused. Thunder? No, the sky was clear. What could it be?

"A thunder-stick," someone said.

Aiee, Red Feather thought. Of course. Like the weapon that cut down poor Never-Speaks.

"Has the attack begun?" he asked.

"It should not be," one of the young horse handlers spoke. "They were to wait for the sun."

Something was wrong, then. Someone had mistaken the plan, or they had been discovered, or any one of a number of other things had happened. And now the town was awake and on guard. This was not good.

Red Feather began to trot forward, toward the increasing murmur of noise that rolled out toward them. The sun began to peep over the rim of earth, and now there was the sound of many running horses, from within the town.

"The horse soldiers come!" someone said.

They could not see the activity in the town, but could hear. There was no question when the detachment of dragoons met the attackers in the street. Red Feather could hear shouts, yells, and the scream of an injured horse. Once he thought he recognized the blood-curdling war cry of the People, but he could not be sure. The noise was too constant, growing across a wide front. He could see others advancing on the town, from other quarters. A musket boomed, some distance away, and the rising tide of the sounds of battle continued to grow.

Red Feather was pushing forward, feeling the urgency to find his companions from the prairie before they were hopelessly involved in the fighting. A figure staggered toward them from the direction of town, bleeding profusely from a saber cut across his shoulder. The man's face showed confusion, and his eyes lacked comprehension. Even as Red Feather looked, the wounded man fell forward to lie face down in the dust.

Another still figure lay in the street ahead, and Red Feather stared in unbelieving recognition.

"Gutierrez! *Aiee*, Enrico, my friend!"

He knelt, to assure himself that there was nothing that could be done, and then moved on, trying to sort out his confused thoughts. The trader had plainly been killed by a musket ball, probably the first shot they had heard. Red Feather, like the others, could not understand why Gutierrez would be struck down by his own people.

"*Aiee*, an evil day," he muttered to himself.

One encouraging thing was the absence of any of Turkey Foot's party. It was known that Gutierrez had traveled with them. Probably they had entered the town together. Red Feather could not imagine the conditions under which the trader had been killed, but it seemed likely that he had still been with Turkey Foot and the others at the time. If there had been other casualties in that first clash, there would be more bodies in the street. So, Red Feather concluded, the others were still alive, at least when they left this spot. They would have moved on . . . but where? Frantically, he tried to think it out . . .

Turkey Foot's primary goal in Santa Fe now was to free Red Feather and his son. At least, Blue Corn had said so. Without the trader to guide them, Turkey Foot would be looking for the jail. Possibly he already knew the location, near the square. Yes, surely that was the answer. The rescue party would make its way to the square, fighting its way if necessary. Even as he reached this conclusion, Red Feather was moving at a trot toward the center of town. There were people, men from the pueblos singing, shouting, searching for someone to attack. Repeatedly, a warrior would look long and hard at the obvious outsider who trotted past. Then they would assume him to be an ally, and perhaps wave a greeting.

A flash of motion caught Red Feather's eye, and he turned, barely in time to see the rush of a soldier in uniform. The man carried one of the long knives, and wore the marking stripes of a sub-chief on his arm. A sergeant, unhorsed and separated from his companions, now fighting for his life.

The saber whistled through the air, dangerously close to Red Feather's ear as he ducked to avoid the slash. There was no time or space to loose an arrow. The knife at his waist seemed to be in his hand of its own volition, and he struck upward into the soft triangle below the breastbone. He felt the knife sink deep, and strike solidly. The startled expression on the sergeant's face faded almost instantly to one of puzzled noncomprehension as Red Feather withdrew his weapon. The soldier fell heavily. Red Feather stepped across him to pick up the long knife. He had never used one, but it balanced well. It would be more useful in this sort of fighting than his own weapons. He sheathed his belt knife and moved on toward the square, the saber ready in his right hand.

A young man of the pueblos darted from a side street, pursued by two mounted lancers, probably part of the dead sub-chief's command. The youth dodged a lance thrust and rolled, almost under the horse's feet. The lancer rushed past his target and wheeled his horse for another run. Red Feather thought of his own son, about the age of this pueblo boy, and ran forward to assist. The other lancer was lowering his weapon for a thrust when Red Feather entered the fight. He swung the saber at the bridle rein as the horse thundered past him. The taut leather strap parted, and the pull on the other rein signaled the horse to turn right. The thrust missed, but the first horseman was whirling back into the fight. To make matters worse, a third lancer now came pounding down the street.

Red Feather still carried his bow in his left hand, with an arrow on the string. He could not use both a bow and the saber, however. The youth had now scrambled to his feet, and Red Feather tossed the bow to him. He had no idea whether the young man could use it well, but he hoped so. There was no alternative, because the attack was now from both sides. He turned to meet the most dangerous charge, forced to trust his companion to protect his back.

The horse with the severed bridle rein was floundering around with no control. It would be a few moments before that rider could either regain control or dismount to fight. Red Feather faced the charge of the newcomer. He edged nearer the corner of one of the adobe lodges, prepared to take cover as he dodged the thrust. But, even with the one animal not well controlled, the odds were not good. He must do something to even the fight. He thought of swinging the saber at the shaft of the lancer's weapon, but was unsure. He did not know whether that might break the long knife, leaving him defenseless. He hated the alternative, but it was a matter of life and death now.

He managed to elude the lance thrust by dodging behind the adobe wall. Then, as the animal swept past, he swung the saber at its legs. The horse went down, and the rider catapulted through the air to slam to the dirt of the street. That soldier would be out of the fight for a few moments. Red Feather turned to the others.

One rider was swaying in the saddle, an arrow jutting from his throat. The soldier on the uncontrolled horse was trying to guide it with only moderate success by grabbing handfuls of its mane. Even as Red Feather watched, the trooper managed to kick the confused animal into a lope away from the fight.

He turned to the unhorsed rider, who could still be dangerous. However, the downed trooper seemed to want no more fight. He scrambled to his feet and ran like a rabbit. Red Feather looked after the trooper a moment, and then turned to the young man.

"Thank you!" the youth said.

"It is nothing," Red Feather answered. "You have no weapons?"

"I lost my bow, before."

Red Feather nodded.

"I need mine," he told the boy, "but take one of these lances."

He picked up a lance and handed it over, taking back his bow. Now he must hurry on.

The crippled horse was struggling to regain its feet, unsuccessfully.

"I am sorry, my brother," Red Feather said to the animal in apology, "but it was your life or ours."

A merciful stroke of the saber ended the creature's suffering, and Red Feather trotted on toward the plaza.

29

» » »

Toward the center of town, the fighting was heavier. The attackers began to fall back under the fierce defense of the Spanish garrison. Red Feather met more wounded in retreat, but pushed on, searching for any sign of his party. Several times he paused to inquire, but was met with blank stares.

Once, he was certain his search was over. Someone pointed out a sector where outsiders were fighting, and mentioned their skill and daring. Red Feather hurried to the designated area, to be met with disappointment once more. There were, indeed, ten or twelve warriors not native to the pueblos. They were not his people, however, but Apaches from the west. He had not encountered many of these desert nomads before, and found that he could not communicate with them. They were unfamiliar with each other's language, and even the pueblo tongue used by these men was one not understood by Red Feather. The Apaches did not, or would not use Spanish, and in addition, seemed completely unfamiliar with the hand-sign talk of the plains. Angry and frustrated, Red Feather moved on.

He was practically in the center of the town before

he encountered a familiar face. He had begun to realize that in this strange new sort of warfare there were differences from that of the open plain. A man must be cautious about his approach to the corner of any lodge or structure. It was easy for it to conceal an enemy. So, as he approached such a structure, he was ready for the assault of a surprised individual who came around the corner. Both rushed forward with weapons raised, and then paused in astonished recognition.

"Red Feather!"

"Swallow!"

"But you . . ." Swallow paused and looked behind him, as if he expected to see Red Feather approaching from that direction, also.

"I will explain later," Red Feather spoke hurriedly. "Where are the others?"

"Scattered," Swallow spoke with a wave of his hand. "Turkey Foot said to stay together, but we were attacked by the long-knife horse soldiers. We are to meet at the plaza."

Red Feather nodded.

"Then let us go there. Have any been killed?"

"Only Gutierrez. Did you know, his own people killed him?"

"Yes. Tell me about it later. Now, let us find the others."

"Is White Fox free, too?" Swallow asked as they started off.

"Yes, he is with his mother."

"Good. We heard they are killing prisoners."

In all directions now, there were shouts, screams of the wounded and dying, and an occasional volley from the muskets of the Spanish troops. A riderless horse pounded down the street and out of sight, running in pain and panic. The feathered end of an arrow protruded from its hip. They passed bodies in the street, both Spanish and native. One was that of a Spanish medicine man. The priest's right hand had been hacked off. Red Feather recognized the symbolism. Some years earlier, the priests had punished some of the Elder Brothers. For teaching the old ways, they had been flogged, and the right hands of two of them had been cut off as a lesson.

He was sick of the entire thing, sick to his heart, and wanted only to find the others and get out, to get away. Life had been so simple among the People, in the open country of grassland, wide skies, and far horizons. Here, the smell of death was settling over the town and the entire area.

It was the end of an era. Red Feather had had much time to think in the cramped confines of the cell. He realized that, even if the trouble was over, it could never be the same. The people of the plains could no longer make the annual journey to trade, as they had for a generation. It had been a special relationship, depending on a few farsighted people who were gone now. The chiefs among the Spanish, both the priests and others who were in positions of power, were now people who did not understand.

The seasons of trading would no longer be. Metal knives, arrow points, lance heads for hunting buffalo, would no longer be available. They must return to the old ways, using such medicine knives as they still had. Just as the people of the pueblos wished to drive out the Spanish and resume the ways of their ancestors, his own people would be forced to do much the same.

He looked down at the saber in his hand. It had proven itself. Much of the medicine of the Spanish was good. Red Feather could see that, besides the medicine of the metal, there were other things. The strange animals brought by the Hairfaces made life easier in the pueblos. Pigs, poultry, the spotted buffalo that could pull carts and also be eaten, were useful. Not to his own people, of course. Theirs was a different life, one which, this morning, seemed the most desirable goal on earth.

"There is Turkey Foot!" Swallow exclaimed.

The old warrior trotted up.

"*Aiee!* Red Feather! You are free!"

"Yes, let us find the others. We must get out."

Turkey Foot nodded. He threw back his head and gave the long, warbling cry of his people.

"Will they come?" asked Swallow.

"Maybe so. Maybe they will meet at the square," Turkey Foot said.

"Should we go there?" Red Feather inquired.

"I think so," Turkey Foot answered, starting down the street.

The fighting sounded heavier in that direction. Red Feather was relieved to encounter two more of their party, approaching from a side alley. Once more, the remarks of shocked surprise greeted him.

"Never mind, now," he brushed aside the inquiries. "Are there others?"

"Otter is dead," said Bull's Horn. "I saw him fall."

"Where is Yellow Robe?"

"Wounded!" Turkey Foot spoke. "He started back."

"Then we are the only ones left?" Red Feather asked.

They looked from one to the other.

"What about White Fox?" inquired Bull's Horn. "Is he with you?"

"With his mother," Red Feather explained again. "I will tell you all, but now, let us go. We will try to come back for the bones of Otter."

He led the way through the streets, trying to avoid as much conflict as possible. Even so, it was some time before they emerged from the outskirts of Santa Fe and approached the area of the encampment.

Yellow Robe's wound consisted of a clean lance thrust through the fleshy part of the thigh. He was lying on the ground where they had spent the night. He was weak from blood loss, and it seemed doubtful whether he could travel.

"I am fine!" he insisted. "I can ride!"

Turkey Foot drew Red Feather aside.

"He will bleed again," he said simply.

"We can camp here," Red Feather told the injured youth. "You can travel better in a day or two."

Yellow Robe protested, but actually seemed relieved. The others began to settle in and reestablish their camp.

Other wounded were returning now, and a more complete picture began to emerge. The fighting had resulted in a standoff for the day. The Spanish had retreated to the center of town and repulsed the attack. Frustrated, the attackers had turned to killing any stragglers. They slaughtered an entire family whose home was a bit outside of the edge of town, killed their livestock, and burned their buildings.

Most distressing to Red Feather was the talk around the camp fires that night. He had envisioned this as a single attack, over and done before the day had ended.

There was none of this in the talk that evening. Small groups were talking, planning the next onslaught.

With a sinking heart, Red Feather realized that the hostilities were not over. In fact, it seemed, they were only beginning.

30

» » »

Even after the initial carnage, it was nearly half a moon before the siege of Santa Fe was over. That first evening, as the shadows lengthened and the camp fires blossomed in the foothills outside the city, excitement was still at a fever pitch. Tales of the fighting were told and retold. The wounded were praised for their bravery.

Men stopped at the camp fire of Red Feather and the others from the plains, to praise their fighting prowess. This group of outsiders had penetrated farther into the heart of the town than most, and their deeds had not gone unnoticed. They felt it unnecessary to reject the praise, or to point out that much of their success was due to misunderstanding. Their thrust toward the plaza had been in the effort to rescue Red Feather, who did not even need rescuing. In turn, his push was to find the others and prevent the dangerous rescue attempt.

In the excitement of the aftermath, however, it seemed logical to take credit for bravery and dedication. They could do so, yet still quite comfortably withdraw and start for home in the morning.

There were many comments about the death of Gutierrez. Men who had been suspicious of him, even those who wished to kill him, now professed lifelong admiration. The fact that he had been killed by his own people made a tremendous impression. It was taken as an indication of the general untrustworthy nature of the enemy. It became a proof, an example of why it was absolutely necessary to drive such a dastardly people from the land.

They mourned the fallen Otter with the traditional song, and discussed the improbable task of recovering his body. It was finally decided to see what the next day would bring. It was entirely possible that there would be a truce to allow both sides to recover dead and wounded. At least, Turkey Foot thought so.

In this, he was badly mistaken. Among the plains tribes, such an arrangement after a battle would be common. However, in this setting, with a century of abuse and hatred boiling to a climax, such a thing could not be.

After dark, Popé himself visited each camp fire, praised the bravery, comforted the wounded, and urged strength for the next day. His was an impressive presence. It was impossible to remain passive around this man, whose spirit reached out with great strength to touch those of any whom he contacted.

"It is good to have you with our cause, my brothers!" he told them.

Somehow, even though their entire presence was a mistake, Popé's simple remark made them feel strong and proud. The very mystique of the man seemed to make every individual believe that Popé had come for the sole purpose of seeing him. Red Feather, of course, felt it very strongly. The great leader paused, and looked him straight in the eyes. There was a question in Popé's glance, yet a recognition also. Red Feather would always believe that this unspoken thought encompassed the memory of the healing ceremony in the kiva long ago, as well as present events. Popé nodded slightly in recognition, and moved on. At least, Red Feather was certain that the nod was one of recognition.

The brief visit from the Elder Brother had an unusual effect on the men from the plains. Without even a discussion, it was assumed that they would remain at Santa Fe, instead of starting home. One of the party described it much later. It had been as if the presence of Popé made it seem reasonable to fight for him, not as a duty, but as a privilege.

By the next morning, the feeling was not so strong. Red Feather was even a trifle confused as to why he had felt this strange call to battle. It was not his fight. Ah, well, they could help with the show of strength, without plunging headlong into the thick of the battle. It should all be over in another day or two. Then, when the time was right, they would leave.

Once more, this assumption proved to be wrong. The days followed one another, with attacks and skirmishes almost daily. Twice the men of the plains almost decided to leave. They were prevented by another visit from Popé. He said little, but once again his spirit reached out to touch them with great power.

The other event was somehow more disconcerting. Hunting Bear, the chief with whom Red Feather had traveled to Santa Fe, stopped at their camp fire one evening, while they were planning their departure. Packs were being readied, and they were making no attempt to conceal their intention. Hunting Bear glanced disapprovingly around the camp, and frowned.

"You are not preparing to leave?"

Red Feather was puzzled at his own reaction. He felt apologetic, almost guilty, and could not explain it. A trifle irritated, he reminded himself that his party owed no allegiance to this cause. They should have no need to explain to anyone. He bristled indignantly, still trying to appear outwardly calm.

"We must return to our own people, and our families," he said casually. "We will leave in the morning."

Hunting Bear paused only a moment.

"We cannot let you do this." His tone was flat. "If you are not with us, you are against us."

Red Feather felt his anger rise, and started to speak, but the other man waved him down.

"You will not leave. You will stay and fight."

Turkey Foot rose to his feet, belligerent.

"Who will stop us?" he demanded. "You?"

His voice was calm, but deadly.

Hunting Bear smiled coldly. He swept a hand to indicate the hundreds of men camped at fires across the hills.

"They will," he said in a matter-of-fact tone.

With a sinking feeling, Red Feather realized that it was true. If these men did not want them to leave, there was no way to do so. He glanced at Turkey Foot, who appeared poised to strike. The old warrior was ready, if it seemed necessary, to fight their way out. Red Feather tried to remain calm as he spoke to Turkey Foot in his own tongue.

"Let it be, my friend. There is no purpose in spilling blood over this, ours or theirs."

Turkey Foot relaxed only a little, but remained alert.

"It can be settled later," Red Feather reminded him. He turned to Hunting Bear.

"It will be as you say," he agreed. "When do we take the town?"

Hunting Bear smiled with pleasure now.

"I do not know. Maybe tomorrow."

31

» » »

The climax of the siege of Santa Fe came when the surviving Spanish broke and retreated south. The attackers let them go, following closely with a large force to see that they did not try to return. They were escorted in this manner down the river they had named the Rio Grande, all the way to El Paso del Norte, the gateway to the north. In this case it became the gateway back into Mexico. It was later estimated that one in four of the Spanish in the whole region had been killed.

The mortality was probably higher at Santa Fe, one of the major points of attack of Popé's rebels.

Red Feather and his party watched the carnage from the viewpoint of outsiders. It seemed that the first day of the killing had acted in a strange manner on the spirits of the pueblo people. Their centuries-old traditions of peaceful tolerance were shattered by the shedding of blood. Now, as they conquered the town, they went marauding through Santa Fe in a blood-frenzy, killing in random fashion, destroying and burning. The thick adobe walls of most buildings were impossible to burn, of course. But wooden furniture and fences were piled high inside Spanish houses and set on fire to burn the wooden rafters and roof supports. Roofs came crashing in, sending a shower of sparks toward heaven, with cheers and shouts from the onlookers.

It was much like the feeding frenzy of a wolf pack, Red Feather noted. The big gray wolves of the prairie, following a buffalo herd, would separate a lone animal from the others with infinite patience. A lost calf, a sick cow, or perhaps an aging bull, its joints stiffening from the cold of many winter migrations. They would circle quietly, perhaps for days, until the weakening animal could be pulled down. Then, even as the dying creature kicked feebly in its last struggle, the ritual of feeding began. Red Feather had once seen from a distance the slashing, tearing assault on the flesh of the victim, the quarreling over the choice morsels. The sounds alone of such a blood-frenzy were terrifying.

He felt the same now, but with an added dimension. The attack of the wolf pack was a part of the life-plan. The wolves were, in a sense, brothers of the People. Both owed their lives to the buffalo, whose flesh provided life.

This frenzied killing seemed almost senseless. Except for the first day, the men from the plains had managed to avoid most of the conflict, fighting only when forced to it. There was a strong feeling that it was no longer their fight, now that the prisoners were freed. If, in fact, it ever had been.

There was, of course, a hatred of the soldiers. A Spanish soldier, dead or dying, would be quickly seized, stripped, and beaten, possibly castrated or otherwise mutilated. Tongues were cut out, hands and feet chopped off, as the frenzy mounted. Naked corpses were dragged through the streets and tossed into burning houses.

Yet, the most excessive of the blood-crazed behavior was reserved for the priests. Of the thirty-odd Spanish medicine men in Santa Fe, only a third survived to begin the retreat down the river. The followers of Popé, with the pent-up anger of a century, focused their vengeance on these men, who had systematically and forcibly attempted to destroy the religion of the kivas. Captured monks were paraded through the burning streets, while crowds derisively shouted obscene parodies of the liturgies they had been forced to memorize.

"El Señor God, father of the Spanish, is dead," they chanted, "and so is Santa María, their mother, who does not remember who she slept with!"

Priests were flogged, mutilated, and finally killed. Eager hands helped to pile their corpses high on the church altars.

Popé had decreed that all things Spanish must be completely destroyed. Chairs, tables, and all furnishings joined the heaps in the churches. The people herded sheep, pigs, and oxen into the sanctuaries and barricaded the doors before setting fire to the funeral pyres that had once been altars of worship. The livestock that could not be crowded inside were slaughtered in the street.

It was possible to see the beginnings of a rift among the followers of Popé. His more zealous disciples were killing and destroying without hesitation all traces of the Spanish. But here and there was a man who seemed reluctant to destroy a favorite weapon by throwing it in the pyre. Another seemed hesitant to kill the sheep, an animal whose pelt could be used many times while the animal itself remained alive.

Quarrels and accusations arose over whose heart was most dedicated yet most reasonable. There were arguments regarding some of the food plants and seeds being thrown into the fires.

"It was brought by the Spanish!" a man declared, holding a bag of grain on his shoulder.

"No," another insisted, "our people have always had this plant, like the corn and the cotton. I have heard my grandfather tell it."

In all likelihood, there were many wrong decisions during the orgy of destruction. There were errors both ways, before emotions came down from a fever pitch to reenter a world of reality.

Red Feather and the others managed to maintain a detached objectivity in all this. It seemed that there was no strong push to force them to participate in the destruction of the Spanish culture. They were astonished at its magnitude. While sacrifices were common among the People, it was for a specific ceremony, such as the Sun Dance. Much more common was a Gift Dance, redistributing objects of value to those in greater need. Wanton destruction was rare.

Young Bull's Horn had helped, with a certain degree of amusement, to round up livestock and herd them to the center of town. When the killing of sheep began, he had participated, in the spirit of an effortless buffalo hunt. When it continued, and it became apparent that this was merely useless destruction, he withdrew and approached Turkey Foot and Red Feather.

"Is this their way?" he asked in astonishment.

Red Feather thought of the frugal life of his wife's parents, of the calm tolerance of Blue Corn, and of the deep perception and insight of the man. Perhaps it would help to talk to him about all this.

"No, my friend," Red Feather said slowly, "this is not their way. Maybe their way is dead."

32

》 》 》

Red Feather could tell that his wife's father, Blue Corn, was deeply troubled. In the years that he had known this respected Elder Brother, he could not recall that he had seen such concern, such preoccupation, in the leathery face. It was even more apparent now than it had been before the attack on Santa Fe.

It was somewhat puzzling to the men from the plains to see Blue Corn in this state of unrest and apparent indecision. Red Feather knew that the aging Elder had not wholeheartedly favored the anti-Spanish revolt under Popé. There were reasons. Blue Corn had always enjoyed better relations with the Spanish than some. It was partly because of his tendency to avoid direct confrontation. There had been some in Blue Corn's village who followed Popé, some who did not. That was the decision in the council. Most pueblos had voted unanimously to follow the campaign with Popé, but this council was undecided. In a matter of such great importance, a unanimous decision was almost necessary. After much discussion, a plan emerged. Let those who would go and fight, and the others remain to look after the safety of the town.

The council was able to come to a unanimous decision on this point, at least. Roughly half of the young men decided to fight.

And now, it was over. The men from the plains had been permitted to leave Santa Fe, with no hard feelings, as soon as the final collapse occurred. The column of surviving Spanish had moved out on the old river trail to the south, flanked by threatening parties of warriors to see that they did not try to turn back. In this aftermath, Red Feather and his party had made preparations to start home, and no one even seemed to notice.

They had been a few days at Blue Corn's pueblo, making preparations for the longer journey. Because of the long delay, the time spent in captivity and in fighting, Red Feather was concerned about the changing of the seasons. It would be autumn before they could reach their own territory. He was not familiar with the climate of this area, except in early summer.

Blue Corn reassured him somewhat.

"You know, the first trading journey of your people was late, like this. Sky-Eyes and Star did not arrive here until late summer."

"Yes, I have heard so," Red Feather agreed, "but the story also says that they found it very cold on the way back."

"You might take the Desert Trail," Blue Corn suggested. "It is shorter."

The People had sometimes used this alternate route, but it had a major disadvantage.

"Would there be water?"

Blue Corn shook his head questioningly.

"Ah, that is a problem," he admitted. "But I think there is still time to reach your people before the snows. Did not the first traders winter with some of your western bands?"

"Yes, it seems they did. With the Red Rocks band, maybe."

"It will go well with you," Blue Corn said with finality.

It seemed that the discussion was over.

What continued to cause Red Feather some concern was the entire attitude of Blue Corn. Despite his optimistic prediction about the journey home, the demeanor of the man was morose and depressed. His usual quiet good humor was missing. He could be felt to be mourning for the problems of his people, but those should be behind, now. Red Feather sought the advice of his wife.

"I do not know," Moonflower said thoughtfully. "I have never seen my father like this. I fear for him."

There seemed no spark of interest, no challenge of the future. The keen eyes where Red Feather had always seen the look of eagles were now flat and without life.

"His spirit seems tired and old," he told Moonflower. "Does it happen that he could let it die?"

"Yes," she answered with some concern. "It is not usual, but these are not usual times."

They talked at length. Both were reluctant to leave until they could see some change for the better. Red Feather discussed the problem with Turkey Foot, who, of course, was anxious to start home. However, the situation was apparent to him, also.

"We should stay together," Turkey Foot said. "We can wait a little longer. The weather will hold."

Red Feather had almost forgotten that Turkey Foot had been on the first expedition.

"How long before the snows come to the pass at Raton?"

Turkey Foot shrugged.

"Who knows? We could winter here, if we have to."

Red Feather had not even considered that. Surely something would change before it became necessary to make such a decision.

Days dragged along, with no apparent change. Finally, Red Feather came to a conclusion. He must directly approach Blue Corn, and inquire as to the nature of the problem. Moonflower agreed, and with many misgivings, Red Feather left their camp outside the village and approached the lodge of Blue Corn. He did not recall when he had been so anxious about anything. What would be Blue Corn's reaction?

Before he could knock or call out, the older man appeared in the doorway.

"Ah, Red Feather, my son," he greeted. "I am glad you have come. I would talk with you. Come, let us walk."

Red Feather's head whirled. Had the man been waiting all this time for him to approach? No, surely not. He tried to see the look in the wise old eyes. There was still sadness, but perhaps a spark of interest that had not been there before. Had something changed?

They walked in silence on the familiar path along the stream. It seemed that Blue Corn used this as his place to think and talk, to make decisions. Neither spoke until they reached the dead cottonwood.

"Let us sit," Blue Corn suggested.

There was a period of silence, as Red Feather waited. Finally, Blue Corn gave a deep sigh and began.

"My son, I need not remind you that these are evil times."

Red Feather nodded.

"But the fighting is over," he observed.

"Ah, yes, that part. But the trouble only begins now."

"I do not understand, Uncle."

"There is badness across the land, Red Feather. I have heard evil things."

He paused, long enough for Red Feather to wonder *how* he had heard. That had always been a mystery of the mountains, how quickly Blue Corn could become informed of events far away. There must be some simple explanation. Messengers, to carry news from one Elder Brother to another? Sometimes it seemed that . . . His thoughts were interrupted as Blue Corn spoke again.

"Popé has changed," he said flatly.

Maybe Popé was back at Taos, Red Feather thought, and someone had crossed the mountain by the old back trail, with news.

"Many thought that the trouble was over when Popé drove out the Metal People," Blue Corn went on. Red Feather noticed that he used the old Tewa name, "Metal People," for the Spaniards.

"Now Popé demands that all traces of the Metal People be destroyed."

Yes, that had begun in Santa Fe. Red Feather had been startled at the killing of the sheep and pigs. There had even been the question of whether metal tools should be destroyed.

"There was much that was good brought by the Spanish," Blue Corn said sadly. "Many see no need to destroy it all, but Popé insists. The tools, knives, all of it."

For some reason, Red Feather thought again of the

days in Santa Fe, and the aftermath of the battle. Someone had stolen the saber he had picked up the first day of fighting. He had assumed that someone coveted it as a weapon, but it had happened after the fighting was over. Was it a gesture of one of Popé's more fanatic followers, a part of the prescribed destruction?

"This has caused a division among our people, one as never before," Blue Corn went on. "Some of the pueblos are loyal to Popé. Taos, Pecos, Tewa. Others, in the west and down the river, have doubts. Did you know that Popé had a man executed? No? One of the Elder Brothers stood up in protest, and Popé had him killed, right there on the spot. This is not our way."

"What can be done, Uncle?"

"I do not know. One cannot protest, it seems. Popé thinks he is a god. He takes what he wants, and kills those who protest."

He sighed deeply and continued.

"Some of the Western Elder Brothers are thinking of leaving."

"Leaving?"

"Yes, to move their people west, build new pueblos. I have thought of it, but I am old and tired. That is far away, and a hard land."

Red Feather was beginning to see the reason for the depression. The decision faced by Blue Corn was a major one. It would be not only the most important choice of his lifetime, but would affect his people for many generations. From a personal viewpoint, it would mean that Blue Corn would never see his daughter and grandchildren again.

Even with this new understanding of the reasons for Blue Corn's behavior, Red Feather was totally unprepared for the next question. The old man looked him squarely in the eye.

"Is there a place in your country where we could make a new start?"

33
» » »

Blue Corn announced his intention the next day. Immediately, four families elected to join him in the dramatic venture. Others were indecisive.

"I am afraid to stay here, but more afraid to go," explained one man apologetically. "We do not know that country. I could not live in a leather tent."

Blue Corn smiled.

"Who knows what he could do if he must?" he asked gently. "But the thought of winter in a leather tent is strange to me, too. Look, my friend . . ." He stooped and lifted a handful of dirt. "Any place there is earth, we can make adobe blocks for our houses. I would hope to live as we always have. But you must do as you think best."

Blue Corn was not as confident as he appeared. He spent a long time in discussion with Red Feather, with Turkey Foot, and especially with his daughter, Moonflower. She, of all of them, was the only person who had lived in both cultures. Half her life in each, he reflected. Even she could not answer some of his questions.

"I am not sure about the adobe, Father," she admitted. "There is much more rain than here. Especially in the People's Eastern range. Will the adobe wash away?"

Turkey Foot thought that the climate near the mountains was not much different from their present location.

"Some colder in winter, maybe, but your lodges are warm," he pointed out. "But you should go far enough on the plains to find good growing."

"There are those who grow crops, then?"

"Of course!" laughed his daughter. "There are many Growers. We trade with them."

"Will there be a place for us?"

"I think so," Red Feather contributed. "You should not choose a place too near any of them. The Pawnees . . ." He shook his head with a little doubt. "No, we trade with them. We will tell them with dignity where you are, and that you mean no harm."

There was an even more important doubt in the mind of Blue Corn. Would the crops of the pueblo people grow in a strange land? Here Moonflower's knowledge came into good use, as she related what she had observed.

"They have pumpkins, and corn and beans. More kinds than yours. Squash and melons. There are other plants not seen here. A water plant with leaves shaped like an arrowhead. They use the roots."

Blue Corn shook his head in astonishment.

"From the water?"

Moonflower laughed.

"Yes, Father. There is much water farther east."

"But you said . . ."

"Yes, that is true. Too far east, there is more water because there is more rain. You must choose a place that fits both your lodges and your crops. It would be good if you could grow potatoes."

Blue Corn threw up his hands.

"Let us talk of crops we know. What about our cotton?"

Those from the plains looked at each other indecisively.

"I had not thought of this, Father. I do not remember cotton in the People's range. Surely not in the Tallgrass Hills."

"To the south of us, maybe," Red Feather agreed. "Where we winter, sometimes."

Turkey Foot agreed.

"But maybe it is because it has not been tried," he added. "I know nothing of growing, but why not take your seed and try it?"

This had to be the final answer. They would take some seed of every possible crop, and see what would grow most successfully.

It was a time of busy preparation. There must be a supply of food for the winter, and to last until next year's crops, in addition to their precious seeds. Moonflower joined the other women in sewing sacks, filling and tying them, getting them ready to load on pack horses.

Red Feather, meanwhile, spent much time in trying to acquire horses. After all the confusion in Santa Fe, there were horses everywhere whose ownership was in doubt. The men from the plains, both those of the People and their Head Splitter companions, were accustomed to counting wealth in terms of horses. They were a most important factor in the hunting of buffalo and transporting of meat, hides, and possessions. After the loss of the pack train, they had felt impoverished, and had attempted to recover their losses by appropriating as many unclaimed horses as possible. If anyone questioned ownership, they were quick to back down. It was unwise for a minority in a strange country to be too assertive. Especially, of course, in a country seething with unrest and bloodshed.

Even so, they left Santa Fe with a respectably sized horse herd. This stood them in good stead with the new decision of Blue Corn and the other pueblo families. They had much stock to trade.

It was an odd situation. Most greatly valued, of course, were the fine hot-blood horses which could be buffalo runners or, on occasion, war horses. Of lesser value were animals with a more quiet, stolid nature. These were usually relegated to a career as pack animals. In this case, though they had acquired the best hot-blood animals that they could, they now needed pack animals. It was necessary to seek out animals which were actually inferior to the ones they had.

"Aiee!" Turkey Foot exclaimed with amusement. "I have never before intentionally traded *down.*"

Gradually, an acceptable train of pack horses was assembled, along with enough riding animals to accommodate the several families who would make the move. The day was selected for departure.

Just before sunset, Blue Corn walked alone along the little stream for the last time, sat on the old cottonwood trunk, and watched the colors change over the western peaks. It was nearly dark when he returned and without a word sought his bed in the house where he was born.

"It is very hard for him," Moonflower observed as

she and Red Feather snuggled for warmth against the night's chill.

"Yes, I know," Red Feather answered. "But he is a wise man. He will do well."

34

» » »

Blue Corn looked around him at the gently rolling grassland. The lush green of summer was fading now, the grasses beginning to show the muted colors of red and yellow as well as a great range of golds and browns.

"Corn will grow there." He pointed to a low, flat meadow.

Red Feather agreed.

"Yes, the Pawnees grow corn, not far from here."

"Pumpkins, too, I think," Blue Corn guessed. "They have pumpkins?"

"Yes, Uncle. And beans and squash."

It was the Moon of Falling Leaves, but still warm and sunny. Their journey had been a good one, with few problems. They had lost only two days' travel because of rains. On those days they had camped and carefully sheltered the cargo of precious seeds to protect them from the rain.

Red Feather had been amazed at the change in Blue Corn's attitude. It was as if, once his decision was made, he became not only reconciled, but eager to get on with it. The rigors of the trail always left everyone stiff and sore for the first few days. Blue Corn, however, seemed to tolerate that well, and even to revel in the challenge. He shed his age as a snake sheds its old skin to emerge with colors bright and new, and with renewed vigor.

Moonflower was delighted with the change.

"I have not seen him more eager for many seasons," she had told Red Feather. "We will see them settled, and then go on to our band's winter camp."

It was Turkey Foot who had suggested this canyon as a site for the new pueblo.

"It has several names," Turkey Foot said. "Our people call it 'Beaver Creek.'"

"Where are the Pawnees?" asked Red Feather. "Is there not one of their bands near Beaver Creek?"

"Yes, but a day's travel north of here," Turkey Foot explained. "We trade with them sometimes."

Blue Corn was now busily laying out the place in his mind.

"Another field there," he pointed. "Houses along the canyon wall. We can build one now, and all live in it if winter comes too soon. Then build others in the spring. Over there, by the stream, will be our adobe pit. We will start to make the bricks . . ." he paused. "Would it be best to ask the Pawnees first?"

"Maybe so," Turkey Foot answered. "We will take you to see them, while others of your people start to make the mud blocks."

"But let us make camp now," suggested Red Feather. "We can start the other things in the morning, with a new day."

The others agreed, and began to unload the pack horses.

"Yes, a new day," Blue Corn said, almost to himself.

Red Feather glanced over to find Blue Corn still staring at the level strip of ground against the canyon wall. He knew that in his mind's eye Blue Corn was seeing a new pueblo, with a new start.

There was one more thing, the excited gleam in the eyes of the Elder Brother. The "look of eagles" had returned.

GENEALOGY

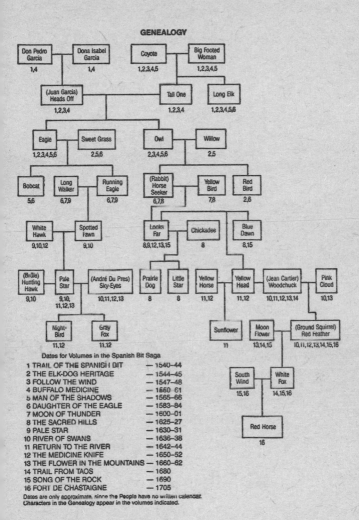

Dates for Volumes in the Spanish Bit Saga

1 TRAIL OF THE SPANISH BIT — 1540–44
2 THE ELK-DOG HERITAGE — 1544–45
3 FOLLOW THE WIND — 1547–48
4 BUFFALO MEDICINE — 1560–61
5 MAN OF THE SHADOWS — 1565–66
6 DAUGHTER OF THE EAGLE — 1583–84
7 MOON OF THUNDER — 1600–01
8 THE SACRED HILLS — 1625–27
9 PALE STAR — 1630–31
10 RIVER OF SWANS — 1636–38
11 RETURN TO THE RIVER — 1642–44
12 THE MEDICINE KNIFE — 1650–52
13 THE FLOWER IN THE MOUNTAINS — 1660–62
14 TRAIL FROM TAOS — 1680
15 SONG OF THE ROCK — 1690
16 FORT DE CHASTAIGNE — 1705

Dates are only approximate, since the People have no written calendar.
Characters in the Genealogy appear in the volumes indicated.

A proud people in a proud land

THE SPANISH BIT SAGA

Set in the New World of the sixteenth and seventeenth centuries, Don Coldsmith's acclaimed novels recreate a time, a place, and a people that have been nearly lost to history. In the *Spanish Bit Saga* we see history through the eyes of the proud Native Americans who lived it.

Turn the page for an exciting preview of **SONG OF THE ROCK**, Book 15 in Don Coldsmith's *Spanish Bit Saga*, to be published in December 1990. It will be available wherever Bantam Books are sold.

Time period: Late 1600s,
a few years after *Trail From Taos*

1

» » »

Perhaps it would have happened anyway, the return to the old ways. Most of the People, however, were inclined to attribute the trend to the collapse of the trading in Santa Fe. For a generation trade had continued, and the People had benefitted greatly, exchanging furs, robes, and sometimes dried meat or pemmican for metal knives, tools, and blankets from the Spanish.

Then came the summer when the men of the pueblos revolted against Spanish rule, and drove the "metal people" all the way back to El Paso Del Norte, in Mexico. The hostilities put an end to the trading, and the People and their allies, the Head Splitters, withdrew to the wide skies of the prairie country.

The return to the old ways was part of the result. It was, in a way, necessary, because the modern conveniences of the metal people were no longer available. It was necessary to revive some of the almost outmoded customs and methods.

Along with this came a renewed interest in the understanding of things of the spirit. In this, the area of religious experience, none showed greater interest than young White Fox, son of Red Feather and Moon-flower.

White Fox had been at a very impressionable age when he and his father were jailed by the Spanish. Hardly fifteen summers, he was taking part in his first trading journey. Only with great difficulty had the party from the plains managed to escape. The bones of two of their number would rest in the strange soil of the mountains, instead of returning to the life-giving sod of the prairie.

All of these things had made a deep impression on the young man. He continued to strive for skill in the hunt, but he also asked many questions. Deep, thoughtful questions about things of the spirit. He talked at great length with his father, Red Feather, and with his grandfather of the same name, the aging chief of the Eastern Band. He sought the knowledge of Pale Star, whose life experience was broader than any other of the People.

With great insight, Star perceived that here was a young man whose spirit cried out for knowledge. She encouraged him to talk with Looks Far, the highly respected medicine man of the Southern Band. The old man was pleased to see a youngster of his own band take such interest, especially one who was practically family. Looks Far had seen with alarm the trend away from things of the spirit, as greater interest in the trade route to Santa Fe had permeated a generation. He had been almost pleased over the collapse of the southwest trade.

And now, he was greatly pleased. He hoped that this interest would blossom and bear fruit. He was beginning to fear that no young man would aspire to the office of medicine man. This generation seemed far more interested in trading with the Spanish, and he feared the foreign influence.

It was always a pleasure to see a young person who asked questions. He remembered Pale Star as a child, and how she had asked many questions. Now came this young White Fox. Looks Far was aware of the boy's brush with death at the hands of the Spanish. Sometimes such an experience would startle a person into inquiry as to the nature of things. Possibly, even, White Fox could be one who would receive the gift of spiritual insight, which would make him a medicine man. He could not suggest such a thing to White Fox. The boy would have to seek it for himself. It was possible, even, that if the gift was offered, White Fox would refuse the call. It was not unusual to refuse the honor of such a gift because of the heavy responsibility that it carried.

So, Looks Far realized, he must not push the young man. He would be available to him, ready to answer questions. He might even suggest that White Fox go on a vision-quest. Many of the young men were neglecting that important spiritual experience, in this generation. Their quest followed more along the lines of the southwest trade. Their interest lay in the best knives, lance points, and arrowheads, rather than things of the spirit. A few, of course, followed the old way, and sought their spirit-guide through the fasting and prayer of the vision-quest. Still, it was disheartening that many capable warriors did not.

The time might come when Looks Far could suggest a vision-quest to young Fox, but not yet. It would be better for him to seek it on his own. No one could seek a vision-quest for another, anyway.

So, Looks Far bided his time and watched White Fox

grow, spiritually as well as physically. The lanky frame was filling out with hard flat muscle, the boyish voice deepening. Fox began to have enough facial hair to pluck with the clam shells. Still his curiosity deepened, and he often sought out Looks Far for discussion. Thus the announcement was no great surprise to Looks Far when it came.

"Uncle," White Fox began one afternoon, "I would seek a vision-quest."

Ah, thought Looks Far, it is good. And Fox had even broached the subject himself. Looks Far's heart was full of joy, but he tried to maintain his dignity.

"Yes, my son, where will you go?" he asked seriously.

It would be necessary to go far enough so that no one would accidentally blunder in and disturb the seeker. The band had camped on Sycamore River for the summer after the end of the Big Council. It was an area that they had used before, one of their favorite sites for summer camp. Looks Far was also aware that a day's travel upstream was the locale of Medicine Rock. It was a spiritual place of great importance. It was here that long ago a man called Eagle had spent the winter in a cave. Eagle was honored in song and dance because of his strange spiritual experience at the rock. He had become, not a medicine man, but a skilled storyteller. It was said that he could tell stories of Creation as if he had been there.

Some felt that Medicine Rock was a place of evil, but Looks Far had never thought so. Probably it was a place of the spirits, a sacred place. The People had always refrained from camping too close because of its spiritual nature, and the reluctance to disturb such a place.

These very factors would seem to make it an ideal place for a vision-quest, however. Looks Far waited for White Fox to inquire about a site for his quest. Then he would suggest Medicine Rock.

The young man paused for a long time before answering.

Looks Far was on the verge of asking again when Fox finally spoke.

"I had thought maybe I would go to Medicine Rock."

The old medicine man could hardly contain his excitement. *Aiee,* what a good sign! A sensitive spirit like that of White Fox, in touch with those of the Rock! With difficulty, Looks Far maintained his dignity, and took a long draw on his pipe before answering.

"Yes," he said calmly. "It is good."

2

» » »

White Fox stood on the south side of the river and stared up at the gray cliff known as Medicine Rock. He had never been this near it before, having only seen its dark line in the distance, looming above the tops of the trees along the river. In reality, it was not a rock, but a bluff which marked the river's course along its north bank for perhaps half a day's journey. From where he stood he could see that in both directions, the cliff tapered toward the level of the riverbed.

He scrutinized the face of the rock for a path to the top. He could camp here, he supposed, but somehow he felt that one's vision-quest should be on some high place, from which he could watch the movement of the sun, the moon, and the stars.

Upstream, perhaps a long bow shot, it appeared that there was a rift or crevice in the cliff, and he moved in that direction, chewing a piece of dried meat as he did so. Soon he would begin his fast, but until then, he would need his strength. Still chewing, he put the last bit of meat back in the pouch at his waist. He had a purpose for it.

He crossed the river at a shallow riffle that murmured over white gravel, and stopped to drain the water out of his moccasins on the other side. There was a suggestion of a path along the narrow strip of soil that separated the river from the rock, and he followed it toward the crevice. In retrospect much later, he was to think that there may have been something odd about a game trail in this location. He thought nothing of it at the time, however. He was too concerned about finding a way to the top. He paused to drink his fill, and filled his waterskin.

The trail did lead into a broken rocky crevice which sloped upward into the cliff. It was a wound, it appeared, which might have been hacked into the cliff by a giant ax. The broken fragments of stone which spilled out of the cleft were tumbled out into the river itself, where dark water swirled around dark boulders. The stones were of a convenient size, and he began to climb, stepping from one boulder to the next. Again, it did not occur to him that this game trail was almost too easy. There was dense growth of fragrant sumac and prairie dogwood on either side, but none to impede his progress.

About halfway up, something white caught his eye to the left, and he paused to look. There below him was a pocket in the crevice, tightly packed with bones. Bones of all sizes. A chill caught at him, and prickled the hairs at the back of his neck. What was this strange occurrence? For a moment, he thought of retreating, but common sense held him. There must be some reasonable answer to this jumbled pile of bones. He sat down on a boulder and studied the situation. Meanwhile he began to recognize more bones among the rocks. Buffalo bones, mostly, though he identified a horse's skull. All of the bones were bleached and weathered.

Then he remembered. Aside from the story of the spirit-experience of Eagle, there was another story of Medicine Rock. A generation or two ago . . . what was it? Ah, yes, invaders from the north. Looks Far himself, as a young man, had joined his medicine with that of a medicine man of the Head Splitters. They had decoyed the dreaded invaders to this area and stampeded a buffalo herd to push them over the cliff. Of course! In the ensuing years, the river had carried away or broken to pieces the exposed remains of the buffalo. But here in the crevices and crannies of the rocks, the moldering bones could only lie through the seasons, hidden away from the world.

He wondered a little about the rider of the unfortunate horse whose bones lay below. Had he escaped? Or was he killed, and his body removed? Possibly, even, his bones also moldered beneath the bleaching pile of buffalo remains. Ah, well, that was long ago. He rose, having solved the mystery to his satisfaction, as well as having caught his breath. He climbed on.

He was above the tops of all but the tallest trees now. He could pause and look up and down the river, and the view was magnificent. He was glad that he had chosen this spot for his vision-quest. Its beauty made him eager to begin his fast, to enter into a oneness with the world. He climbed on.

At the top, puffing slightly, he climbed out onto the level stone rim and stood to look around. The immediate area was as flat as still water, and stretched away into the distance with only a gentle roll. Even though the general lay of the land was what he had expected, the appearance was startling. The level flat of the plain came to the cliff's edge and simply dropped off. He could see now how it had been possible to maneuver the enemy invaders into position and crowd them over to their deaths.

The sun was lowering in the west, and he hastened to make camp. A fire was essential, so he began to gather dead sticks from some of the scrubby brush which clung to cracks in the rim of the cliff. He took out his fire sticks, and with the fire-bow twirled the yucca spindle to produce a glowing spark. Carefully he gathered it on a pinch of tinder and breathed it into life. A flint and steel from the Spanish trade would have been quicker, but it did not seem appropriate to the spirit of his vision-quest.

The little fire began to grow as daylight began to fade. He fed it meagerly. It was not necessary for cooking or warmth, but for ceremony. It was a ritual fire only, a declaration to the spirits of the place that "with your permission, here I intend to camp."

He spread his robe, gathering some of last year's dead grass to pad the sleeping-place, and sat down to watch the setting of the sun. He took out his last stick of dried meat and broke it equally in half. One part he solemnly deposited on the fire as a sort of sacrifice to whatever spirits might take notice here. The other he chewed slowly, the last morsel of food he would take until after his vision-quest was over.

The air was still, and the pleasant scent of roses drifted across the plain. The season was good, the grass green. Sounds of the day were fading, replaced by the sounds of the creatures of darkness. A coyote called from a distant hill, and its mate answered.

Below him, a fish splashed in the river. There was

the hollow cry of Kookooskoos, the great hunting owl. How strange, to hear that sound from below him.

Stars began to appear in the darkening blue of the sky, and the world was good. Now, he knew, there was nothing to do but wait. He added a few twigs to the fire, and on an impulse stood to sing the Song of Fire, because it seemed an appropriate thing to do. Then he settled back down.

He did not feel sleepy at all. He was far too excited. The light faded to the strange blue-purple of twilight, which distorted not only distance but reality. There was an air of expectancy, a sense of some supernatural event about to happen. Then the great red disk of the full moon edged its way above earth's rim to the east, and the feeling of wonder and mystery was complete.

The red circle had shrunk to half its size and turned to silver overhead before White Fox finally drew his robe around him and lay down to sleep. He was a little disappointed. There had been nothing out of the ordinary. Only the accustomed night sounds and the silvering of earth with moonlight.

He lay waiting for sleep to come. The last sound he remembered before falling asleep was the slap of a beaver's tail on the surface of the river far below.

3

» » »

White Fox awoke with the rising sun in his eyes, unsure where he was for a moment. Then he remembered and sat up in anticipation. But the magic of the night was gone now. The unearthly silver-blue of the moonlight world had been restored to the normal colors of any pleasant morning in the Moon of Roses. He looked up and down the river, and across the tops of the trees which lined its banks.

Through an opening in the vegetation, he saw a deer tiptoe her way gingerly to the water to drink, followed by a pair of spotted fawns. He smiled. Twins, a good sign. But no, another doe, somewhat more grayish-yellow than the reddish color of the first, came into sight. Ah, one of the young must belong to her. Then to his surprise, two more fawns tottered into view. *Aiee*, what good fortune! What a favorable omen, not only for his vision-quest, but for the season. Any season in which the does are prone to twinning will be a good year.

His stomach rumbled, calling attention to his fast.

"Be still," he said, "you have a long time to wait."

White Fox sipped a little water, and then rebuilt his

fire, starting it from the tiny coals of last night's blaze. He walked to the rim of the cliff and performed the Morning Song, lifting his hands to the sky in the prayer of thanks for the new day. A few more sticks now fed the fire, and he spent a little while gathering more, moving a few steps back down the cliff path to reach a dead bush he had noticed there.

It was about that time that he noticed a strange senation. He could not have described it, a sort of feeling that he was not alone. It was as if he were someone else, and himself as well, standing on the narrow path, his foot on a projecting rock to more easily reach the dry fuel. No, more like someone else had stood just this way. Or, as if someone watched him. He glanced around, half expecting to see someone, but he was alone. Only a bright-eyed sparrow balanced gracefully on a twig and watched him curiously. Watching the teetering bird, White Fox became dizzy for a moment. He leaned hard against the cliff until his head cleared.

What was it? The effect of his fast already? Maybe, he thought. He must be very careful about the treacherous path if dizziness was to be a part of his experience. He gathered the sticks he had dropped, and made his way back up to the rim.

The dizzy sensation was gone now, but there remained the memory of the other feeling, that he was not alone. That was a separate experience, not related to dizziness, and one that was very real. *Aiee,* the spirits of this place must be very active! It whetted his eagerness.

His stomach growled again, and a hunger pang clawed through his abdomen. He took only a tiny sip of water. The waterskin was his only supply, without negotiating the path to the river and back. He hated to think of trying that. There were places on the narrow ledges that were dangerous, even without dizzy spells.

He sat down near the edge and looked again up and down the stream. The haze of fog in the river's bend was beginning to lift now, a thin layer of mist above the water's surface. It was interesting, the way he could see the tree trunks both above and below the layer of fog. Again, he heard the slap of a beaver's tail on the surface of the water. He remembered that from the night. Downstream a band of crows were angrily calling an alarm, and he watched in that direction. Soon a great owl came flying on quiet wings, softly slipping among the trees along the river. *Kookooskoos* was pursued by a raucous horde of noisy crows, who flapped and dived at their traditional enemy repeatedly.

White Fox smiled as he watched from above. The owl did not even lose its dignity. It sailed in a smooth glide, to rise at the end and land effortlessly on a dead snag near the cliff's face. From there it was only a short flight to a crevice where it disappeared from view. The owl's tormentors circled and cried in protest for a little while, but their game was over. They soon fell silent and went their separate ways.

White Fox, a little bored, settled back to wait. He was hungry, but that was expected for the first day of a fast. It would pass. For now, until he began to benefit from the anticipated visions, he would simply observe the world and enjoy it.

From this vantage point, as the fog melted and disappeared, he now found that he could see much of the river's course. It curled in deep pools against the dark gray of the cliff, murmured over white gravel bars, and among the knobby knees of the giant sycamores that knelt at the water's edge. He wondered idly just where the cave was located, the winter abode of the legendary Eagle. Did the injured youth look down on this same scene, the chalk-white bark of the sycamore there? Did the leaves of that very tree, a giant of many winters, murmur in conversation with the stream while Eagle listened, as White Fox listened now? He realized that he was thinking in abstract terms, but after all, was that not the purpose of a vision-quest?

A beaver splashed again. Was this beaver family descended from those heard by Eagle as he lay in his cave, generations ago? White Fox studied the river again. It was ideal for beaver. The deep pools made it unnecessary for them to even build a dam. He had not seen a beaver lodge as he approached last evening, but often the animals merely used a den in the riverbank itself in such a setting. Life would be easy here. The explosive slap of a tail on the water sounded again, and he smiled. It was startling, the loud crack of warning that the animals could make as they dived. It was apparent that many times there was no real danger, that the warning was only in play. The beavers could apparently alter the sound of the slap to fit the urgency of the situation.

He lifted his gaze to watch a red-tailed hawk, circling with fixed wings on the rising air that lifted as the sun began to warm the face of the cliff. It was good, he thought, to take these days to merely watch and learn of the earth and how its creatures lived. Maybe this was the goal of the vision-quest. But no, there must be more, a great deal more. He had had no visions yet. He wondered if they would come as dreams, the visions of sleep, and if so, would he be able to remember them when he woke? Sometimes such night-visions seemed quite real, and every detail could be remembered. Sometimes it was possible only to remember fragments. Then there are the terrifying night-visions that one sometimes has, when it is good to waken. He wondered what the effect of the fast would be on all of these. Looks Far had repeatedly mentioned the clarity that the fast brings. Would it help with the memory of the dreams? Or, would the vision-seeker be in an entirely different state, seeing and experiencing visions while not asleep?

He sighed deeply. He must not become impatient. It would come to him in due time, but he must wait for the effects of the fast. He had not dreamed at all last night.

But wait, he thought suddenly. Did I not dream? Was there not a time, after the moonlight turned silver-blue, when I woke . . . no, I was not awake, but I heard the beavers, and . . .

Flitting through the cobwebby recesses of his mind was an unclear picture, which seemed somehow to be part of his presence here in this place of spirits. There was, somehow, an interfering presence, a disharmony that had intruded, to jar the calm of his now-forgotten dream. He closed his eyes and strained to remember, but it was of no use. The memory of the fragmented dream was much like that of reality, the moonlight on the river, the night-sounds. But he had a strange partial recollection of something more ominous, something not a part of the night of magic. A face came into his memory, not remembered clearly, but in brief partial pictures. Long, unkempt hair, large burning eyes, and an expression on the face that was midway between fear and fury.

He opened his eyes in alarm. He was not even certain that this face was human. For an instant he thought of abandoning his vision-quest and fleeing this strange place, but then he calmed. He had never heard of anyone who abandoned a vision-quest. Certainly, not when it had hardly started. He would be ridiculed forever.

Besides, was it not the purpose of the quest to approach and learn of things of the spirit? He took a deep breath, and the cold prickling sensation at the back of his neck seemed to subside somewhat. In the clear air and the warming light of the sun, the chill of fear that had washed over him for a few moments seemed ridiculous.

Still, he wondered, is this thing of fear a part of the vision-quest? A gnawing doubt remained.

About the Author

» » »

DON COLDSMITH was born in Iola, Kansas, in 1926. He served as a World War II combat medic in the South Pacific and returned to his native state where he graduated from Baker University in 1949 and received his M.D. from the University of Kansas in 1958. He worked at several jobs before entering medical school: he was a YMCA group counselor, a gunsmith, a taxidermist, and for a short time, a Congregational preacher. In addition to his private medical practice, Dr. Coldsmith is a staff physician at Emporia State University's Health Center, teaches in the English Department, and is active as a freelance writer, lecturer, and rancher. He and his wife of 26 years, Edna, have raised five daughters.

Dr. Coldsmith produced the first ten novels in "The Spanish Bit Saga" in a five-year period; he writes and revises the stories first in his head, then in longhand. From this manuscript he reads aloud to his wife, whom he calls his "chief editor." Finally the finished version is skillfully typed by his longtime office receptionist.

Of his decision to create, or re-create, the world of the Plains Indian in the 16th and 17th centuries, the author says: "There has been very little written about this time period. I wanted also to portray these Native Americans as human beings, rather than as stereotyped 'Indians.' That word does not appear anywhere in the series—for a reason. As I have researched the time and place the indigenous cultures, it's been a truly inspiring experience for me."

★ WAGONS WEST ★

This continuing, magnificent saga recounts the adventures of a brave band of settlers, all of different backgrounds, all sharing one dream—to find a new and better life.

☐	26822	**INDEPENDENCE! #1**	$4.50
☐	26162	**NEBRASKA! #2**	$4.50
☐	26242	**WYOMING! #3**	$4.50
☐	26072	**OREGON! #4**	$4.50
☐	26070	**TEXAS! #5**	$4.50
☐	26377	**CALIFORNIA! #6**	$4.50
☐	26546	**COLORADO! #7**	$4.50
☐	26069	**NEVADA! #8**	$4.50
☐	26163	**WASHINGTON! #9**	$4.50
☐	26073	**MONTANA! #10**	$4.50
☐	26184	**DAKOTA! #11**	$4.50
☐	26521	**UTAH! #12**	$4.50
☐	26071	**IDAHO! #13**	$4.50
☐	26367	**MISSOURI! #14**	$4.50
☐	27141	**MISSISSIPPI! #15**	$4.50
☐	25247	**LOUISIANA! #16**	$4.50
☐	25622	**TENNESSEE! #17**	$4.50
☐	26022	**ILLINOIS! #18**	$4.50
☐	26533	**WISCONSIN! #19**	$4.50
☐	26849	**KENTUCKY! #20**	$4.50
☐	27065	**ARIZONA! #21**	$4.50
☐	27458	**NEW MEXICO! #22**	$4.50
☐	27703	**OKLAHOMA! #23**	$4.50
☐	28180	**CELEBRATION! #24**	$4.50

Bantam Books, Dept. LE, 414 East Golf Road, Des Plaines, IL 60016

Please send me the items I have checked above. I am enclosing $_____ (please add $2.00 to cover postage and handling). Send check or money order, no cash or C.O.D.s please.

Mr/Ms _____

Address _____

City/State _____ Zip _____

Please allow four to six weeks for delivery.
Prices and availability subject to change without notice.   LE-3/90